Dorcas the Invisible Cleaner

JD Cooper

Those who cling to perceptions and views wander the world offending people." -Bhudda

=

"Life is really simple, but we insist on making it complicated" - Confucius

=

"Be nicer than necessary to everyone you meet. Everyone is fighting some kind of battle." – Socrates

Dorcas the Invisible Cleaner

Intro - A beautiful day

It was a beautiful sunny day in Sandford, the birds were singing, the sun was shining, and a slight early morning breeze rustled only the smaller leaves in the trees. This was a day which I thought should be celebrated with wise words - words which showed that they had been thought about, words which meant something, and which said today would still mean something tomorrow.

``Morning Dorcas, gonna be a belter !" pontificated my neighbour.

"Without doubt Derek, without doubt" I replied.

Words to live by Derek, well thought out and so unlike yesterday when he said that exact same thing, and the day before, and the day before that...oh wait, he did change it up a bit last week though

"Morning Dorcas, gonna be a scorcher" Derek had said last week.

He hadn't been wrong about the day, it was just that I thought he should try more, try harder, think perhaps a little deeper and not get caught up in the banalities of life - that was just a cop out I thought.

'A cop out' - now that was a strange expression, I wonder what made me think of that. I know that to cop out meant an evasion or an escape from facing up to something, but that it actually came from the Scottish term - to 'cup out' or 'empty your cup' - bloody Scots, everything had to be about drinking with them.

What was a 'cop' in' then? I'd have to ask when I get to work - my new job starting strangely enough at the police station - maybe subconsciously that was what made me think of 'cop out'.

I knew a lot about words - I loved them, I believed that without words you couldn't really communicate with anyone, obviously, but I mean deeply, in a life changing way and that had been my mission since I'd left school - to reach, no, to connect with at least one person a day.

I hadn't really connected with many people in my younger days, apparently, I had been 'a difficult child' according to the nuns who raised me. I didn't think I was difficult, just that I asked a lot of questions, and they didn't always have the answers. I'd never been one to accept the first explanation I received, and I would always have a 'come back', a 'rejoinder' if you will. It wasn't that I was being rude, argumentative, or unappreciative of the nuns having taken me in at birth and having tried to educate me, it was just that I really wanted to understand how things worked, how their minds worked, and I don't think they were used to children questioning their authority.

As I had grown up, I will admit I had a few 'challenges with authority' as was the term. As a teenager I had had the usual run-ins with the police, which was quite scary, but not as scary as being brought home by them to the nuns. It didn't matter whether I had done something wrong or not, whether I was guilty or innocent, the nuns stood with their heads bowed as I entered, like a reluctant firing squad and formed a line from the front door directly to Mother Superior's office.

As I passed each nun I got more and more withering looks, or despairing looks, but the worse was the disappointed look usually given to me by my favourite nun - Sister Bernadette. That really hurt, especially if I actually hadn't done anything wrong.

I did learn a lot from the nuns, apart from the usual educational subjects of maths, English and so on, they taught me about religion, about their beliefs, their acceptance of a higher power. But whilst they taught me and I understood their explanations I never believed, as they did. I could not accept there was anyone looking down, over me and everyone else in the world - what? All at the same time? It just didn't make sense. No, they were just trying to explain what a conscience was.

One of the Sisters though - Sister Bernadette, privately taught me what I would always regard as the best subject, for it spanned everything, and in fact was the basis for many other disciplines The name of this subject was - philosophy.

Philosophy is often described as either the study of the fundamental nature of knowledge, reality, and existence; or as a theory or attitude that acts as a guiding principle for behaviour. They both sound as though someone has sat and thought and then made up a load of words to sound clever. Personally, I prefer the literal definition of philosophy as simply 'the love of wisdom', and I think Sister Bernadette also preferred this description though she would never admit it publicly. I often got into trouble at the children's home on purpose so that Sister Bernadette, who often took the detention classes, could teach me about our 'love of wisdom'.

Sister Bernadette gave me books on the subject and introduced me to people who would never leave me. These were mainly men, mainly old men, mainly old Greek men, and all of whom happened to be dead. I know it doesn't sound the cheeriest way to spend an afternoon - reading about old dead Greek men but trust me once I'd read some of the classic books by these masters I was hooked. I didn't understand half of it and disagreed with the other half and maybe that was the point, maybe you were made to disagree on purpose, to make you think more deeply.

When I left the children's home I did so because of an opportunity I had been given. I was a clever child, and I easily passed the exams I was set.

This led to more exams and eventually I left for good to go to university on a full scholarship. I had been given an exciting opportunity, the nuns said, to go out into the world and ask my questions. 'Preferably of someone else' Sister Bernadette had smiled at me.

I had a few issues at university, but I will tell you about those later. It does no good to live in the past, you can't change it, you can only regret it. As a little chubby bloke, I know once said, 'do not dwell in the past, do not dream of the future, concentrate the mind on the present moment' - and he wasn't even Greek - he was Indian, but goodness was he deep.

So, I left university with a top exam result but then didn't know what to do with myself and so I sort of fell into cleaning. I'd clean houses for people who didn't know how, or just couldn't be bothered, and I would clean office blocks - they were good to do as you found all sorts of things just kicking around, just thrown away by uncaring, unthinking people. Eventually though I found a place I liked for a while, it was at a local bank, and I found a man there who I liked as well. Oh, not in any physical way, I wasn't interested in men for that, I'd been let down too many times and thought them a waste of time. No, my friend at the bank was a bit of a thinker like me, although we differed in our lines of philosophy. Many nights we would sit and talk and try to convince the other that we were right, that we had 'the answer', when in truth neither of us did. My friend's name was Trevor but more about him later.

I had always thought I needed to 'get on' in life and mundane things bored me, they took up too much of my valuable time, time I could use more profitably. All I wanted to do was sit and think but I knew that this would not pay the bills and so rather than expend my energy on a skilled job I took menial jobs, like the cleaning, to free up my mind for its true purpose - thinking. I needed very few possessions and money in itself held no allure for me. I knew it could get 'things', but what were 'things' but baggage, and the way I lived, I needed very little baggage.

And then I saw the advert in the paper that was to change my life. It read:-

WANTED !

FULL TIME CLEANERS

TO WORK AS PART OF A SMALL CLOSE-KNIT TEAM

FOR A FORWARD THINKING, MODERN ORGANISATION

FLEXIBLE HOURS, COMPETETIVE PAY

For more information, please contact Suzannah Dowling (Facilities Manager)

Sanford 654805

Starting a new job was an exciting opportunity, a fresh beginning and I knew that I must seize this particular opportunity with both hands.

As my old friend Demosthenes said 'small opportunities are often the beginning of great enterprises'.

I still had to do my other cleaning job at a local bank, but I'd managed to drop that down to three evenings a week, and that had allowed me to take on this new role, as the Head Facilities (Maintenance) Manager at the new and sprawling police station. I had heard things about the new building and the people who worked there, and I had formulated a plan. But perhaps as my plan was to conceive a crime it was probably a plot or may be a scheme. Either way I was on the way to start a new adventure - there you are, an adventure, that sounds less…criminal.

The new police station was a four-storey grey monstrosity plonked delicately on the edge of town. It was situated out of the high street naturally, where it would have obviously been way too big, but useful if you needed sanctuary having been robbed or buggered on a Friday night. Where it was, was just far enough out of the town that people didn't bother the Constabulary too much with nonsense like reporting crime or asking advice. You'd really have to mean it to go that extra mile to see the face of Her Majesty 's finest.

I'd met the Facilities Manager the previous week - a lady called Suzannah Dowling, and initially I hadn't much liked her. I thought Suzannah (with a z and an h don't forget) was a little too big for her immaculate leather boots, but fair play to her. This was the seventies and there weren't many women in top jobs, but no doubt that would change in time. Perhaps one day only women would be in the top jobs. Perhaps one day those who appointed people to top jobs would look beyond the attributes one person had over the other, their obvious qualifications for the role being applied for and just appoint the best woman for the position.

But I knew I was just dreaming, that day would never come, men wouldn't allow it, surely?

I walked along the deserted street and wondered if five o'clock really was a decent time to have to set off for work. Once I'd got my feet under the table, I would ask my staff what time they thought best to start work. I appreciated that it was a police station I was going to work in, and police stations were a twenty-four seven kind of business, and ergo it didn't really matter what time I started (what a great word ergo was). Suzannah had told me at the job interview that I would be working with a small but tight knit group of people and that I could move things around to 'facilitate objective differential groupings'. I had thanked her for her kind words and didn't feel the need to point out that that particular group of words was nonsense, literally making no sense whatsoever regardless of which way a person tried to facilitate them. Or that perhaps Suzannah should be more pauciloquent- let her work out what that meant, I had to look it up the first time. Or remember that 'silence is better than unmeaning words' - turns out that Pythagoras said that. Wasn't that the triangle bloke I hear you say? Yes, and I have a theorem about that - ha ha!

Anyway, when I got to the police station, I was met by the night turn Desk Sergeant. I knew this was a chance to make a good first impression and that you only got one chance to make a first impression.

It was possible that the night turn Desk Sergeant had a different view to me, or that he didn't get many opportunities to make a good first impression on people he met. Either that or the first impressions they made on him …lasted. I'm sure he saw the worst of people, or at least people in their worst moments and perhaps he had seen too many over the years to worry any more.

D   Good Morning Sergeant, what a wonderful day it is today,
I am Dorcas….

DS   Oh, thank fuck for that, get the kettle on love, I'm gasping

D   Yes, certainly, only it's my first day and I don't know where anything is, let alone the kettle. I'm supposed to be meeting Suzannah Dowling

DS   Good luck with that Dora, she won't be in till about nine

D   It's Dorcas but what's in a name? That's unfortunate about Suzannah, what shall I do until then?

DS   Sorry, Dorcas I've no idea, but I quite agree though, about the name thing, by the way I am Sergeant Bob Fitzwilliam - yes, I know, I didn't choose it, the surname I mean. But I don't get any stick here for that moniker I can assure you

D   Oh? I would have thought….oh I see, sarcasm

BF   You get a lot of that round here Dora

D   Dorcas

BF   And you can call me Fitz. Kettle's through there

And so, I now assumed the role of tea maker for the night turn staff. There weren't that many of them, so I didn't really mind, and as I didn't apparently have any access to my office until nine, I didn't have anything else to do. I wondered where the rest of my staff were, it was now half past six and surely all of them couldn't be late or have gone sick.

Looking around the station
and meeting the boss

I wandered around the police station with the ease of someone who wasn't really there, a ghost, an ethereal spirit, and thought that this could really be a fantastic opportunity for a wicked person, a bad person, or even a thinking person like myself, as I did not consider myself wicked or bad.

I opened doors and cupboards and said 'good morning' to anyone I met and was greeted with early morning grunts or nods - but then again, I was only the cleaning manager, why should they waste their valuable time chatting to me - I was a nobody, I didn't really exist in their world and could have no effect on them whatsoever.

During my interview with Suzannah, I had to answer the usual questions on the form - age, height, weight, place of birth etc, but I had not been asked about my past. I was sure that they would have checked to see if I had ever been in trouble with the police, to see if I was an axe wielding homicidal maniac for instance, and probably as thoroughly as to see if I had ever had any parking tickets, but no one had asked me about what I thought, about anything. It was a very brief interview.

SD What makes you want this job, Dorcas?

D   It pays well, and I need the money

SD Anything else

D   I understand it's shift work and that's good for me as I have to do two
    jobs just to survive

SD You'll have to drop the other job Dorcas

D   But if it doesn't interfere with my ability to perform my duties here is that
    a deal breaker?

SD It isn't a deal breaker, but I would want your assurance that you would
    look to drop that job as soon as possible in all the exigent circumstances

D   Exigent? Well yes, in that case exigent, obviously meaning severe, pressing, oppressive, taxing, exacting, demanding, imperative, then yes, I would look to immediately work towards a meeting of your facilitation led enquiry in the immediate and short-term future bearing in mind my own personal circumstances as a new member of the team and

	work with you to achieve contingent timeframes and objectives
SD	Perfect. Then we understand each other
D	Indubitably and without any presence of incomprehension or misapprehension
SD	So when could you start?
D	Monday?
SD	Excellent. Oh, just one other thing. Do you know anything about management?
D	You mean, treat people well, make sure that they are well motivated and happy in their role, whilst making informed and decisive decisions and balancing the needs and objectives of the organisation to achieve successful outcomes for all stakeholders? No. Not a thing
SD	We'll send you on a course
D	Thought you would

And that was it. They hadn't asked me about what I thought about working in the police station, or even what I thought about the police as an institution, nothing.

I hadn't had to sign any confidentiality agreement and had just wandered into the station early one morning and walked about like I knew everyone.

When the early turn came in at seven o'clock, I wandered down to the front desk, as it was one of the places, I knew had a kettle and quietly made myself a cup of tea. Milk and two sugars - I'd brought my own supplies. The tea bags here would have to go as it seemed the local practice was for them to be used and reused and perhaps not surprisingly there weren't any left in the tin, and no one had thought to bring any in with them this morning.

The two Desk Sergeants exchanged greetings, one in the inward coming way of a person not wanting to be here in the first place, and one in the outgoing way as befitted someone who had so many better places to be. I watched this hand over and noticed also that the waste baskets, for which, when I actually started work, I would be responsible for emptying, were crammed full of paper, probably important paper and that no one seemed to care about security or confidentiality, which was strange for a police station if you thought about it.

The early turn Desk Sergeant turned to me
and asked

DS   Are you the new cleaner love?

D   I think so, but I haven't done a great deal
of cleaning and I've no idea
where my office or anything else is at the
moment. I was supposed to be
meeting Suzannah Dowling when I got
here at half five this morning, but
apparently, she's not often here till nine?

DS   If you're lucky - snooty cow that one -
FLAPS. Anyway, kettles over there.

D   Yes, I've got one....I....FLAPS?

DS   Milk and three sugars love - ta.

D   Certainly, I've just the tea bag for
you, sweetie

And so, I reused a night-turn tea bag, waved it
lightly but lovingly at the Sergeant's teacup,
which I thought, to save on the washing up you
understand, could probably just as easily be
reused from last night as well. Placing it lightly
but lovingly at the Desk Sergeant's elbow I
wished him a pleasant day and strolled away to
see exactly what was in the wastepaper basket.

I had been honest with Suzannah. I was not an axe wielding homicidal maniac, and as I had never owned a car, I had no parking tickets or other motor related skeletons in my past. I had answered honestly all the questions I had been asked and offered nothing else. I had been taken on in the bank in similar circumstances - they needed a cleaner and I could clean. Everyone was happy. Certainly, having worked at the bank for some years, I was very happy, and there had been no complaints from the bank yet, so presumably they were happy as well.

I went and sat in a conference room with the contents of the wastepaper basket. It was still only about half past seven and so there was no chance of any senior officers coming in just yet - they would still be lounging in their dressing gowns in their suburban houses with their Geraldine's, or their Monica's and reading the Telegraph or the Guardian or whatever broadsheet they had delivered. The police were no different to businesses. The workers worked and the managers dicked about and pretended to manage, so I knew I had about an hour.

I worked quickly with the paperwork and found that some really stupid people threw away some really important documents, probably without thinking. No. That wasn't fair. It wasn't stupidity, it was complacency. If you dealt with confidential things every day and got used to that being the norm, then you often failed to see their importance in isolation.

And that situation presented an opportunity for the careful person, the unseen person, and who in any large organisation was the most unseen person....the cleaner.

The careful person would never steal anything physical, and so the careful person would never be caught with anything that could incriminate them or lead to difficult questions being asked of them, and I was nothing if not careful. I had my own system of recording information, my own special language. If anyone found my little notebook it would seem like the ramblings of a mad old lady, either that or a very specific shopping list, and it had served me well for many, many years.

And so, I recorded all the information I had culled from the wastepaper basket and noted it all down in my little book.   After that I put everything back and was just picking up the wastepaper basket in the conference room when the door opened.

"Who are you?" "What are you doing in here?" boomed the incoming man who was dressed in enough braid to cover three tunics let alone his own bulging one.

"Oh, hello young man, I'm Dorcas, the new Facilities (Maintenance) Manager, I'm having a little look around to make sure I know where everything is whilst I'm waiting for Suzannah Dowling - the Facilities (Facilities) Manager, she was supposed to meet me this morning at half five, but she hasn't come in yet, so I thought I'd start seeing what my staff do, and what I can do to help....Why are you laughing? Are you laughing at me?"

"For fucks sake woman, FLAPS has really had you have over, hasn't she? You're not very bright are you. The 'Facilities (Maintenance) Manager - really? That's like calling a doorman an Egress Liaison Consultant - you're a cleaner pure and simple, just that, nothing else, a fucking cleaner, woman. You have no staff, you are it. I'd get cracking if I were you, it's a big nick you know"

"May I ask who you are young man, a man young enough to be my son, and yet one with a rude capacity to point out another's faults whilst ignoring their own"   I enquired

"I am Chief Superintendent Colin Bradshaw. This is my police station and like my own little country I rule it. I rule it as I see fit and I can hire and fire whoever I want. Just remember that before you speak to me"

"Oh, it's like that, then Colin, is it? Well as Epictetus said 'when you are offended at any man's fault, turn to yourself, and study your own failings. Then you will forget your anger'. And its 'whomever' knobhead"; and with that I left the conference room with my head held high, two wastepaper baskets in my arms and a shed load of shopping items to look over in my little notebook.

Chief Superintendent Bradshaw however remained standing where he was when he had first entered the room. But his mouth had changed from its usual snarling grimace to being locked in the open gape of one who had just had his arse handed to him, and by a cleaner no less. If he ever met this Epictetus bloke, he would fucking lamp him.

Meeting my actual boss

As more people were arriving for work my wanderings were a little restricted and it probably wouldn't look too good to be wandering around, introducing myself as a cleaner and well, not cleaning. I was a little disappointed to hear what that overblown lump of lard had said to me about not being very bright, for I was very bright, but maybe being seen as a bit thick would play into my hands. I was pondering this when the lift opened and a woman walked out, nose in the air and bumped straight into me, spilling a cup of coffee she was carrying all over the carpet.

"You fucking idiot, woman, watch where you're going, you've spilt this expensive coffee all over me and the carpet....oh wait, Dora, you're the new cleaner, that's handy, clean it up immediately and then see me in my office".

"It's Dorcas, as you know Sue, since you hired me, and if I knew where the cleaning stuff was, I would willingly clean your mess up". I replied before I could stop myself.

"It's Suzannah, with a z and with an h, if you remember, and please address me as that, or Ms Dowling" snorted Suzannah

"And it's Dorcas with a D and an O and an R C A S. I will see you in two minutes, and don't forget 'when you point your finger at someone three fingers are pointing back at you' "

But Ms Dowling had already flounced off in the vague direction of the Senior Officers conference room and may not have heard my pithy quote.

As promised two minutes later I knocked and entered Suzannah Dowling's office. It had the feel of a Parisian brothel I thought, in that there were swathes of pastel-coloured drapes at the windows, a far too deep purple shag pile on the floor and lounging settees where perhaps office chairs should be. There was also a lingering smell that I thought, as a cleaner, would be a challenge to locate and then eradicate.

D   You wanted to see me Madame
SD   Ms
D   Pardon?
SD   Ms. I've told you before its Ms. Ms Dowling

D   I'm sorry, I don't know what Ms means. Is it like Miss, or Missus?

SD   No it is not, and that's the point isn't it. It's not either of those titles - it shows that I am an independent woman who is in charge of her own destiny

D   Oh, right. Then I suppose I must be a Ms as well then. I've never been married, never thought titles mean too much really and as far as destiny is concerned, I have always thought as Heraclitus said that 'character is destiny'.

SD   Who on earth is Heraclitus, what are you going on about?

D   Well, that's the point about him isn't it, no one knows too much about him, he only wrote one book and that was lost, so we only know what other people wrote about him and what he apparently said. He actually predates Socrates

SD   Look. I don't know if these people are friends of yours down the pub or whatever people of your class have, but I wanted to speak to you about your role here.

D   Oh. I think I know my role here. I am to manage a 'small, but close-knit group of people'

SD   Yes. Well. There may have been a slight oversimplification of what you thought I said in your interview

D   No. No. I made notes, did you want to see

SD   No. That's fine Dorcas. But I need to explain your actual role here

D   I am a cleaner....no, sorry....I am the cleaner, the only cleaner, correct?

SD   Yes.

D   And you knew that would be the case when you interviewed me ?

SD   Yes

D   And you knew that I had to drop three days working at my other job to make sure I could work here?

SD   Yes. But to be fair, I did say you would have to drop that job entirely if you wanted to work here, so it's not like I'm taking money off you or anything, I was quite clear on that I'm sure you will agree.

D   You were not truthful with me. Veritas odit moras, Ms Dowling

SD   What? Oh dear, have I hurt your feelings Dorcas - that was never my intention, it was purely business I can assure you

D   As one of 'my mates down the pub' once
        said 'I choose not to be harmed
        and therefore, I won't feel harmed. If I
        don't feel harmed, then I haven't been'
SD   Deep
D   So, where do we go from here? I would
        prefer to stay working here, well actually,
        I would like to start working here, seeing
        as I've been here for the
        the best part of the morning already. But
        if I may be honest with you for
        a moment?
SD   Certainly
D   I always give people I meet three chances
        in life. You have just used one of yours.
SD   Meaning?
D   Meaning that you lied to me, actually
        gave me a job under false pretences and in
        the process lost me money. I think that
        qualifies as one chance lost
        don't you?
SD   Well perhaps I wasn't entirely clear on
        what your role would be, but perhaps you
        should have asked more questions

D   Oh? So, it's my fault? I tend to agree with the concept that you should 'never let your sense of morals prevent you from doing what is right' don't you?

SD   I have no idea, I've never really thought about it

D   Anyway, are we finished? Life can only be understood backwards, but it must be lived forwards. Don't you think?

SD   Again. Not really thought about it, Dorcas. Sorry.

D   Could you point me in the direction of my office please. You're not
      looking at me....it's a cleaner's cupboard, isn't it?

SD   Yes. Sorry. Here's the key.

D   Understood. Not unexpected.

I left the Parisian brothel boudoir and headed downstairs in search of the smallest cupboard door, a door which I hoped would open up to a wondrous array of expensive cleaning products, gadgets and apparatus which would only enhance and assist my daily role in this fine new expensive building.

With what could only be described as nervous anticipation I slowly slid the key in the door lock and stood back awaiting a gold mine of detergents, soaps, and cloths.......and nearly cried when I saw a tatty old mop and bucket staring back at me.

I knew where the money had been spent, I had seen reclining settees in an office, I had seen the rosewood conference table and wondered how many more unnecessarily expensive items there were within the police station, whilst essentials went unpurchased. I picked up the mop and bucket and decided to start my day. Fortunately, today was not a bank cleaning day as, now I knew I was on my own, I would most likely end up taking all day cleaning the building.

Thinking only of the opportunity life had presented me with, I recited one of my favourite Heraclitus quotes - "He who does not hope for the unexpected, will not find it" and I was determined not to lose hope and to definitely find the unexpected.

A bit about my past

And so, I set off to clean the police station from top to bottom, or, rather, I decided, from bottom to top. There was little point in pulling the tails again of the two tigers I had met so far. The Chief Superintendent and the Facilities Manager were not people I wanted to upset, or even have to deal with too often. I needed to be oblivious to them, silent and unseen, whilst still being indispensable.

At the bottom of the police station was normally where the cells were and so, I set off for there. I could probably gain a lot of information and therefore knowledge from a little light dusting and a little proper tea making in the right areas. I liberated some tea bags from an office on the way down to the cells and took my mop and bucket with me. The Custody Sergeant greeted me warmly.

CS   Awa pet, howya din?
D   Sunderland? Newcastle?
CS   Near enough. Gateshead. What about you pet, where are you from?

D	Oh, here and there. Nowhere in particular really
CS	Everyone's from somewhere. I'm Terry by the way. Terry McDermott, and if you say 'like the footballer' I will lump you, first day or not
D	I don't watch football, Terry, so it wouldn't mean anything to me. How did you know it was my first day?
CS	Walls have ears Dorcas, walls have ears
D	And they make very nice ice cream too, I'm told. I must get on. Is it OK if I have a bit of a dust around?
T.M	It would be like painting the Forth bridge, but you carry on. Fancy a cuppa?
D	Oh, that would be lovely, milk and two sugars please
T.M	Yep. Me too, kettle's over there

I made Terry and I a decent cup of tea with the liberated tea bags and realised that I would have to be careful with him. I hadn't had anyone call me by my current name straightaway and that made me suspicious. Best keep the quotes down a bit and play the thick card whilst down here. The custody area might be a dangerous place, and not just because of the people brought in kicking and screaming in handcuffs.

I had a long-term plan, and I knew I should do nothing to jeopardise that, especially so early on in my 'police career'.

Throughout my first day I gave everything a light dust and a quick mop, and made it seem that what was already clean was now gleaming. I was cheerful with everyone and went about my business with an air of efficiency that surprised even me, and while I cleaned, I looked and listened.

What I did as well was tidy up - little bits of paper that fell from desks or found themselves kicked under tables, and I noted down all the information contained on them in my little notebook.

Eventually it was five o'clock and I thought I had had a long enough day for anyone and that it was time to go home. So, I packed away my extensive cleaning products in my cupboard, put on my coat and headed out towards the front desk.

D   Good night, Sergeant. Have a quiet one
DS   Night Dora, look after yourself

That's it, no one knows me, no one sees me, just like I like it, I thought.

As each day passed, I became more of a feature at the police station, more people called me 'love' or 'pet' and actually acknowledged my presence, even if it was just to lift their feet up so I could sweep and mop around them, and some people occasionally thanked me, although only one called me by my name, or rather the name I was currently using.

I had a curious past. I had not always been Dorcas Goode. I had been so many other people but currently I liked being Dorcas Goode. It suited what I was doing at the moment.

When I had left Nottingham University some years ago, I had been Catherine Taylor and that had also suited me just fine at the time. It was a simple name and simple names were easily forgotten by so many people. That was the name on my philosophy degree and that was the name I would go back to when everything had worked itself out. For that name had a history, that name had a grounding, and that name would do just fine. But for the moment Dorcas Goode would do - it had a lovely ring to it I felt.

When I was Catherine Taylor, I was at one of the best universities in the country. I studied hard, played hard, and enjoyed myself. There were the endless lectures and the usual all-nighters, where you learnt a lot about your fellow students, their strengths, their weaknesses, and their capabilities. It was easy for me to spot weaknesses in people, what made them tick and more importantly what made them crack, when and where I could exert pressure on them, to gain that little advantage I needed to get ahead. Without boasting I thought I had a bit of a talent for it but playing mind games with a few Uni students was one thing, but it was never going to pay the bills and it was never going to get me ahead in life. These people had no real money, they would spend loads but it all belonged to Mummy and Daddy or the taxpayer. I wasn't a nice person then, and perhaps I am not a nice person now. I admit I used people to my own advantage, but, well, why not. These people were not my friends, these people would not be in my life any longer than the three years of a degree course and perhaps a drunken week in Zante to celebrate. No, they would be straight back to Mummy and Daddy and suckle at their teats for the next few years, whilst pontificating about how well educated they were and how the world owed them a living.

I had used these people as practice. Practice for the real event. It was easy then to walk into a bank with a utility bill and a passport which contained a picture which looked roughly like you and deposit a few pounds to open the account up. The cashiers were not particularly bothered and if you chatted a bit to them, maybe showed a bit of cleavage to the young lads on the till then it was simple.

I think I probably opened accounts at nearly every bank in Nottingham and had a steady stream of other people's money coming into them for almost all my three-year stint there. I wouldn't say I made millions, but I was definitely okay for money, which most students couldn't say they were.

I didn't feel bad about any of it. Students thought they were clever and many of them were, but none of them were street wise. There is a massive difference between intelligence and cleverness. So many people no doubt passed their degrees with flying colours and probably went on to have fantastic careers in their chosen fields, but at the back of their minds was me. Who was that strange girl that we used to knock about with? Cathy? Katie? Karen? They would always wonder what had happened to their grant cheques that term, what had happened to their passport when they were due to fly off to go skiing with Mummy and Daddy in La Plagne or Val d'isere.

For me it became a bit of a challenge but also almost an addiction. I couldn't help myself. The greater the risk, the more excited I was by the challenge and as the money kept rolling in, I have to admit it did become a bit of a way of life.
I wasn't fleecing someone every day but when a new student joined our little group or came into my view, I set myself the challenge, the task of finding out what made them tick, and how I could take them into my confidence and locate
their weaknesses.

I remember one girl who came into our little group, and who had assisted me in my studies, her name was Nadia. She was bright, pretty, and very outgoing, and all the boys loved her. We seemed to hit it off almost straight away and often studied late into the night. That was my best time, night-time studying - a time when intelligent but not clever people let their guards down, a time when a searching question could be thrown in with all the others, the 'Well do you like Phil or not?', and the 'I know, but did you see the look on Steve's face when you said that?'.

I would wait until answers were literally pouring out of someone and then ask something like 'but, how do you cope, going to all these parties, they must be so expensive?'

And Nadia had said those three little words that people like me just love to hear….'my trust fund'.

From that moment Nadia became my best friend - she had been a close student acquaintance before, as I never got too close to people, and never, ever allowed anyone to get close to me. She had just moved into the top three fellow students I would happily 'do absolutely anything for!' as we always said in Halls.

Over the next few weeks Nadia and I were inseparable, we had the same classes, so it was easy to keep her in my sights, but after classes we ate together, drank together, and went to the same gigs and so more and more she started to trust me.

I had to bide my time in this venture, I had to wait for the right moment to strike, and eventually that moment came.

We had all agreed to go to a gig in town, I can't remember who was playing, some local bands and a one hit wonder headline act no one could really remember.

About ten of us met up in a local pub and started to have a few drinks. At that time, I was 'poorly' and so I only had lemonade - I had to keep my wits about me.

Being Uni students some of us had to have proof of identity when buying a round and a glorious moment arrived around ten that evening. Nadia bought drinks for everyone and was carded and as her proof of age she produced her passport....hallelujah!

So now all I needed to do was find out where she banked and borrow her passport for a short time.

We didn't look unlike each other, but I had a few photo booth pictures I would be able to swap over for my purposes. I couldn't afford the risk of being challenged with what I hoped would be a large withdrawal.

Nadia had been somewhat disappointing, or rather her 'trust fund' had been somewhat disappointing. I think, like me, she made herself out to be someone that she really was not.

CT.   Good morning, I'd like to make a withdrawal from my account please?

Cashier.   Certainly Miss Tereshkova, how
                much were you wanting?

A silence fell over the banking hall, or at least the
little part I was in

Cashier.   Miss Tereshkova?

I hadn't realised the cashier was speaking to me
as I was a little taken aback by the balance, he
had shown me and was still staring at the flashing
white figures on his green computer screen.

Nadia's 'trust fund' turned out to be a figure of
speech and was in fact a Barclays bank student
account with just over one hundred pounds in it.

Even though I was sorely tempted out of spite to
take the whole lot I couldn't bring myself to do it.
Why spoil a beautiful friendship for the sake of
one hundred pounds?
'Fifty pounds please' I said to the cashier and
handed him the withdrawal slip.
Nadia had just slipped out of my top three
favourites, no more late nights, no more study
help, I thought she could forget that, and I started
to avoid her, I started to be unavailable when she
came round to my room. I know I was in the

wrong, I know that it was me that stole from her, but I was cross with her. Why hadn't she been the heiress she portrayed to be, why hadn't she been worth my time and effort. I decided to move on from Nadia.

This sort of behaviour continued for me throughout my time at university, and I admit I wasn't proud of myself. It paid the bills, and no one really got harmed. Oh, there were a few upset people on the corridor phone moaning on at their parents to send more money as they 'absolutely couldn't survive on just their grants, could they?' At the time I thought, not one of them considered getting a part time job to help their cash flow issues, not one of them, and it made me cross. There I was funding myself through Uni and what extra money I managed to scam off a poor little rich kid was, by comparison, chicken feed. I used that money to entertain others, not for me to survive.

I look back on those Nottingham days as me developing educationally not only as a person but as a con artist, for that was what I was. I was and am to a certain extent still just that, but I am at peace with it. We all lie to other people nearly every day and to ourselves even more often.

Who can, hand on heart, say that they are truly honest with themselves, let alone other people. Every day I say that I will stop, turn to the light, do the right thing and then something comes along needing my attention, needing money thrown at it and so I use the skills I have to resolve my difficult situation. Last month it was the roof, the month before a burst boiler and without using the skills I possess I would still have a leaking roof and a burst boiler.

I think of these things I do as necessities in my life. As I have said before I try each day to reach one person, to make a good difference in their life, and I probably do that to counter the wrong I am doing to some other poor soul in theirs. Sort of balancing the books as it were. I think everyone does it subconsciously but that most people give up.

Anyway, hark at me, getting all dark and meaningful. I am a cleaner and a con artist in my spare time, or is it the other way round, I sometimes forget.

But I do not consider myself a bad person. I always go for someone who either I think can afford a little loss, financially or, as in many cases I think deserves a little reckoning in their lives. I'm no better than anyone else and don't ask for any sympathy from anyone. I have a game plan and when you find out what it is, perhaps you'll not think of me so badly. At least that's what I hope.

As I've mentioned I worked three evenings in a bank in the next town up before I got the job at the Police Station, and I did enjoy it there. I had an 'in' at the bank, someone sympathetic to me and my seemingly lowly position as a cleaner. This person's name was Trevor, and he really was a nice man. Oh, don't worry I never fleeced him, firstly because he didn't have any money, and secondly because he was a good, decent, and kind person. To him I was Cath the cleaner and we could always have a good old natter over a cup of tea.

I first met Trevor when I opened my account at the Midland Bank in town. I needed somewhere to deposit my cleaning wages and I thought it the most convenient. Fewer questions would be asked of me and my past and it just felt right, sort of being loyal to my employer. I had never used the Midland Bank account for anything nefarious and all was as it should be for a cleaning lady and her finances.

Money went in and money went out, nothing too elaborate or eye catching....not yet anyway.

In talking to Trevor, I feigned an interest in banking whilst I cleaned around his feet and those of his colleagues who also came in early or stayed late. Again, as I did at the Police Station, I looked and listened. I have a good memory and I didn't write anything down in my little notebook until I was alone.

Trevor wasn't the brightest chap in the world, and he let a lot of things slip that probably, on reflection perhaps he shouldn't have - systems, timings of things and also where people's spare access cards were kept. Not access to doors and things, I didn't need that, I was already in the building – no, these cards were to access the computers. But I am getting ahead of myself.

Trevor had opened my account for me - well, when I say, me, I mean Cath Taylor, me. Everyone in the bank knew me as Cath and provided my two jobs did not cross over then all would be well. The police had asked for a reference, and they had been duly supplied with one. You have to remember this was the seventies and the way you did things then was by letter. A letter was sent to a would-be referee, and a reply was returned extolling my virtues as a cleaner. I went into the bank early each day until the letter from the police arrived and used bank note paper to reply after a few days. I think they've probably tightened things up now, but at that time things were very lax.

As so I now had two jobs doing what I did best, and that wasn't cleaning. To be honest I was a terrible cleaner, but I tried my best and made things look about right on a regular basis, and there weren't too many complaints.

Busted

As was my wont, I pottered around in the Custody area. I found it comforting and even when Terry was not there it seemed to be what proper policing was about. There was a feel about the place, an energy - not always a good energy, but it had a soul, which was not present in the offices, there was a feel to those places, but it wasn't an energy, it was almost a presence, and not a good one. I wondered how many people had had their futures decided over a late-night kebab, or a bottle of scotch and the toss of a coin - I would never know

T.M Awa pet you got a minute

D Yes, Terry, what's up

T.M Bit private, through here, yeh?

D Yes, now you mention it the interview room does need a bit of a clean. Too many late-night cups of tea spilt all over the walls perhaps.

T.M No perhaps about it, that'll be DS Fairbourn - fat bloke, upstairs, sweats a lot?

D   Oh yes, lot of cleaning near his desk I can tell you, not the tidiest of people Terry

T.M   No, and in a way that's what I want to talk to you about Dorcas.

D   Oh right, why's that?

T.M   Dorcas, I look, I listen. I say nothing. Sort of Zen, me

D   Right…meaning?

T.M   Zen, Buddhist like, silent but deadly you know

D   'Beware the quiet man, for while others speak, he watches, and while others act, he plans, and when they finally rest, he strikes'

T.M   Or she, Dorcas

D   Not with you Terry. The anonymous quote says 'he'.

T.M   Yes, but in these enlightened times, I think we can accept that the gender quoted is not the key issue contained within those wise words is it, Cathy.

D   Terry?

T.M   It may be that you and I can work together for good, what do you say?

D   I take it you don't mean to make the world a cleaner place, do you?

T.M   You are a terrible cleaner Dorcas, but just what you're up to I haven't quite worked out yet.

D   I could give you a load of old guff about I had to change my name due to a violent ex, or someone who just wouldn't stop stalking me

T.M   Or that you are trying to put together a new life following your childhood traumas in a care home

D   But you know the truth Terry

T.M   What is the truth Dorcas - 'Vitam impendere vero' - dedicate your life to truth

D   Latin Terry? Truth Terry? You're a Custody Sergeant in a Police Station

T.M   And you are a cleaner Catherine Taylor. What do you say, shall we work together for good? Shall we combine our knowledge of others to take them down? Not for profit but for the greater good

D   A sort of utilitarian approach

T.M   Precisely

D   How would it work? But first of all, how did you know?

T.M   Your fingerprints Dorcas.

D   I've never had them taken. That silly woman upstairs told me to come down here and have them taken, but on the way down I forgot.

T.M   Yes. I know, but you cleaned most places down here, but the place you didn't clean was the place you'd just touched. And like they do on the tele I 'dusted for prints' and sent them off for matching. It took a while as I had to wait behind all the unsolved murders, rapes, and robberies but eventually they came back, and it confirmed what I thought.

D   Which was that I was Cathy Taylor

T.M   That you were Cathy Taylor, formerly of HMP Walworth and before that Nottingham University

D   And you're not Terry McDermott are you

T.M   No. I bloody hate Newcastle United, I'm a Forest fan through and through.

D   And your real name is Steve Markham, ex-partner of supposed Russian heiress Nadia Tereshkova.

SM   And a Latin degree holder. Yes. Little cow she was, she bitched and moaned about losing fifty quid out of her bank account, which I presume was you?

D   Yes, sorry.

SM   And all the time she was putting out that she was an heiress, while not putting out if you get my drift

D   Too much information Steve, sorry, Terry if we are to keep up appearances

SM   Anyway, To business. I won't drop you in it, and I take it we can go to work?

D   Hang on. Are you actually a copper at all?

SM   Oh yes, absolutely. Went to some shit Training School down here and I never looked back. I've thoroughly enjoyed my time in the police, but the bottom line is, that while I've always tried to do the right thing, others have shat on me, trampled on me, and generally fucked me over so many times I've sort of had enough. I'm due to retire shortly so I couldn't believe my eyes when you waltzed in here bold as brass. And I started to think who is the person that everyone ignores, who is the person that no one notices and can go anywhere without being doubted

D   The cleaner

SM   Precisely. So here is my plan. This place is rotten from the bottom up, Custody Unit excluded naturally

D   Naturally

SM   And I would like to do something about it. I haven't got time left to do things the proper way, and some people may have to get hurt to get rid of the wronguns, are you with me?

D   Definitely

And so, Steve, sorry Terry, told me his plan. It wasn't that far away from my own plan, and I thought they could both be worked on together. I'd have to juggle a few things here and there, but I was on board with what he wanted and perhaps he didn't need to know everything about my plan.

A bunch of Neanderthals

In the nineteen sixties police forces realised that with the massive rise in drugs across the country, the police would have to respond before it got out of control. The idea was to form intelligence led groups of officers in all forces, who could share information cross border and that way effectively follow criminals across county lines. The hope being that through shared intelligence it didn't matter where the arrests were made so long as the police won, and the criminals lost.

What actually happened was that county Drugs Squads were formed and rivalries began. In the modern parlance, dick swinging exercises were commonplace and neighbouring forces routinely withheld vital information from one another to hopefully get the arrests on their ground. This obviously led to criminals getting wise to going across as many borders as possible and effectively widening their operations whilst the police kept theirs as small as they ever were. The criminals' dicks got bigger and the polices' shrivelled.

What also happened more and more was not just that some officers were sampling products they seized from criminals, (with the obvious effects on people not used to taking drugs let alone drive at speed or complete complicated paperwork), but that they also saw an opportunity to make serious money. Officers all over the country took bribes and looked the other way, or they intimidated criminals with threats of arrest or violence.

The police station I was now working in was, apparently no better than the rest. The Drugs Squad, I was informed, consisted of a Detective Sergeant - the aforementioned DS Frank Fairbourn; two hairy arsed Detectives called Baz Sturgess and Vince Donohue - I had to laugh as their initials were BS and VD, probably very appropriate for their role, and I nearly fell of my stool when I heard of the Drugs Squad probationer was called Larry Stevens-Davies - LSD, I kid you not ! There were others who came and went, brought in to help with big cases, but they hadn't been seen recently and not a lot of work seemed to be going on in this office when the core staff were about.

My anonymous informant told me over a cup of tea in the Custody Unit that I should take an interest in cleaning there, as God knew it needed it and that he would work on other avenues of taking down the whole Unit. I personally thought this was a bit of a tall order and my approach would be a little more direct.

The Drugs Squad office was on the third floor, well away from other mainstream offices and had the air of a truck stop cafe when I first went in there, 'to clean'. There were teacups on nearly every surface, and these were filled almost to overflowing with cigarette butts floating in a brown liquid, which may once have been tea though smelt strongly of urine - Christ knows what men do when they're caught short. I know what women do, they nip behind a bush, but it would appear that these Neanderthals couldn't even lope the twenty yards or so to the toilets at the end of the corridor.

Where there weren't teacups there were plates, no wonder poor Ida in the canteen was always running out of crockery. Plates everywhere with half eaten bits of what was once toast, fish and chips or pies. The smell was absolutely vile, but no one seemed to notice, they just moved things off their particular surface and carried on like it was all normal.

I formulated a plan for this particular office but first I would have to, I must, tidy up, actually do my paid job.

I went back downstairs and found some large bin bags in my cupboard which had, to be fair, started to be stocked at my request with proper cleaning products, so Suzannah with a z and an h wasn't perhaps all bad.

I returned to the office and having done a recce found the weakest of the Neanderthal herd

D   Excuse me Larry, is it?

LSD   Yeh babe, that's me name

D   And mine is Dorcas

LSD   Cool

D   Cool. Do me a favour Larry would you?

LSD   Whatever you need sweetheart, name it, I'm there

D   Hold this bag for me would you deary

LSD   Drugs is it, that type of bag?

D   No, it's not a drug bag. And I know only one of us here is wanting to be a Detective, but you would need a shed load of drugs to fill this particular bag, wouldn't you?

LSD   Better look in Baz's desk then darling,
       hadn't you?
D   Listen you little shit, hold the fucking bag
       open when I tell you to, stop with the
       puke making epithets as I am old enough
       to be your grandmother, and maybe, just
       maybe you'll walk out of here with your
       pimply fucking face intact. Get the idea?

My new best friend and I then went around the
office, me with my broom and Larry, Sweetheart,
Stevens, Babe, Davies, Fuckwit, holding the bin
liner open when directed and trying not to gag as
cup upon piss filled cup and plate upon plate with
their gelatinous contents were swept lightly but
firmly into it.
Having thanked him profusely and having asked
him to deposit the bin liner in the skip downstairs
for me, as I had 'terrible sciatica', I returned to the
now relatively clean office and began my
pretend cleaning.

I had to make it look like it was general cleaning,
and now that I could see empty desktops, I saw
the scale of my task.   This place hadn't been
cleaned in a very long time and I would need to
do some actual cleaning to justify my time in the
Drugs Squad office.

I set about hoovering and polishing and dusting and wiping until the place looked less like a truck stop cafe and more like a police station office.

Larry had just returned from the skip.

LSD   Excuse me, would you like a cup of tea?

D   What? No babe, no darling?

LSD   Look, I'm sorry about that, I thought the Skipper was in his office and I needed to sound like I belonged here. I don't normally talk like that , I'm normally very quietly spoken and honestly, I am usually quite polite

D   OK Larry, I'm prepared to give you a chance. Milk and two sugars please

LSD   Oh? I thought ? What with you being the cleaner and all?

D   No. Cleaners clean. Coppers drink lots of cups of tea, and if you're making one for yourself then I'll have one as well. Please.

LSD   Right you are . I'll be right back.

And true to his word Larry, the would-be Drugs Squad Detective who only wanted to fit in, came back a short time later with two steaming hot teas and four slices of buttered toast. He'll do for me, I thought.

LSD   Here you are

D   Dorcas

LSD   Dorcas? That's

D   Weird, strange, Curious?

LSD   Unusual. It's an unusual name. Where does it come from?

D   My imagination

LSD   Ha ! Good one !

D   I think we should be able to call ourselves anything we like, shouldn't
       we? Our parents call us what they think sounds good, but it's not what's
       good for the child, it's what they think sounds good, do you see what I mean?

LSD   Not really

D   Let's say, for example, that I was born to Mr and Mrs Stacey. They might think it would be fun to call their daughter Tracey, you know, just to be
       different, unusual.

LSD   Tracey Stacey - yeah, I sort of like it

D   Yes, but you wouldn't if you had to live with it would you. I mean it's like these hippie types who call their progeny silly names, which they think are all mysterious and spiritual, I don't know like Moonflower, Silver Star, Earth Shadow, things like that.

Oh, they might be all groovy and trendy when the little baby is looking up at his mother in their forward-facing hemp papoose and all, but when little Moonflower Silver Star Earth Shadow is thirty-eight and still working behind the pick and mix at the local Woollies, well, it sort of loses its mystery, its allure, if you will, don't you think

LSD   Well yes....but are you saying....

D   No. Larry. I am neither Tracey Stacy, nor Moonflower Silver Star Earth Shadow. I am just Dorcas. Dorcas the cleaner.

LSD   OK. I understand

D   Really?

LSD   No, not really

D   Perhaps I should just do a bit more cleaning Larry. Thanks for the tea and the toast. My shout next time, eh?

LSD   It's a date

D   No it's not

So, I got to work, actual work, actual cleaning and as I was working my way around the office, sweeping under desks, emptying bins and so on I kept my eyes open.

Larry had been in the office on his own and he said he had to pop out to see a snout, whatever that was, and so I found myself alone in a supposed corrupt Drugs Squad office.

One of my first finds was a printout from a computer. Computers had been installed in many of the offices and whilst I didn't know exactly how to use them and certainly not for police purposes I could read. And what I read was someone's history, someone's life story, criminally speaking.

This particular person had started their criminal career at a very young age, a bit of shoplifting, a bit of petty theft and so on, and then progressed, if you could use such a term, to burglary. This printout told of their life going rapidly downhill and now at the apparent age of thirty-five someone for whom life seemed very difficult. Their latest brush with the law seemed to be an arrest only a few weeks ago for drug possession, and so I supposed the reason for the Drugs Squad officer to have this particular print out. What I couldn't work out was the reason that the printout had been taped to the underside of DC Baz Sturgess's desk.

I took a note of the name and address contained within what was termed this person's 'previous' and put them back where I had found them. I would ask Terry what he thought was going on there.

I got back to cleaning, and just in the nick of time (if you'll excuse the pun) as, in walked DS Fairbourn and DC's Sturgess and Donohue.
I had had a bit of an inkling that they were about to enter the former truck stop cafe as I both heard them and smelt them coming down the corridor. The smell was a mixture of Old Spice, Brut and kebabs. The language was... well Neanderthal

BS   Honestly Skip, this bird last night was a
        right goer
DSF   Oh, go on then Baz, what happened
VD   Yeah Baz, what happened, was she...you
        know was she...

I couldn't see the hand gestures, but I could imagine what they were trying to describe
BS   Oh yeah, enormous mate,
        absolutely enormous
VD   Where did you take her then

BS   Oh, I went 'old school' mate. I took her to the Little Shangri La on Coombe Street, you know the one, the one with the tablecloths, right posh.

VD   What did you have for dinner then

BS   Supper, you fucking ingrate, when its past seven o'clock it's called supper

VD   Alright, keep your shirt on, what did you have for supper then

BS   Prawn cocktail for starters, obviously

VD   Obviously

BS   Then we had something called a 'fondue'

VD   What the fuck is a fondue

BS   It's classy, it's sophisticated. What they give you is all your meat, cut up in little chunks and they bring a pot of boiling oil to your table. You then
use these skewer things to dip your bits of meat into the boiling oil until they're cooked, and then you can dip them in runny cheese and into the boiling oil again

VD   Why?

BS   Why what?

VD   Why do you have to do that, didn't they have a cook?

BS   A chef Vince, he's called a chef at a posh restaurant

DSF   Had the night off, did he?

BS   No, it's posh, its sophisticated

DSF   Its fucking stupid mate, that's what that it

VD   And you pay for this?

BS   Of course you pay for it, it's not free, is it?

VD   But you're doing all the work, shouldn't they pay you?

BS   Just fucking listen will you

VD   Sorry Baz, go on

BS   And to finish we had had something called chocolate mousse

VD   And was it alright, all of that, did it pay off, was she swept off her feet

BS   No, actually it was fucking horrible. The prawn cocktail was alright, you can't go wrong with a prawn cocktail, but the bits of meat kept dropping off the skewers and I had to keep fishing them out of the oil, the cheese just formed this huge mass of, well, boiled cheese , I had four chips, half a dozen peas, and a load of fucking cold sauce all over the edges of the plate. The chocolate mousse was like a dog had barfed it up yesterday and no, Vince, just so I'm being honest with you, it didn't pay off. She walked out after the mousse and told me she was going for a kebab, and I didn't see her after that

VD   Oh Baz, sorry to hear that .... enormous
        though were they
BS   Enormous Vinny my old son.
        Fucking enormous

The three suave and debonair Detectives walked into the office and saw me.

They looked like they had been up all night, and probably hadn't shaved or bathed in about a week. They each wore frilled open shirts, way too tight gaudy coloured trousers and the clunkiest heels you've ever seen, not on a racehorse.

I didn't know if this was standard dress for Drugs Squad officers or not, but the smell surely couldn't be usual. No wonder the woman had walked out after the mousse, she probably couldn't stand the smell anymore.

DSF   Alright love, kettle on? I'm gasping
D   No. It's not, I'm afraid, I've spent half the
        morning cleaning your pit of an office, it
        really is a disgrace you know. I've not
        stopped, so I'm sorry but you'll have to
        sort yourself out
BS   Yeah, he's used to that love
VD   Bit like you had to then Baz, after that
        bird walked out on you !

I had to leave the office before the combined reek of the aftershaves knocked me out. I had the rest of the station to clean, and I had spent a lot of time in here, for not a lot really. I would go and see Terry and see what he thought about the paperwork I had found.

Terry greets a guest, and mad PC Harris

D   Morning Sergeant McDermott, would you have a moment to speak at all?

T.M   Certainly Dorcas give me one minute to deal with this guest

I then saw why the Custody Sergeant's position is the best and worst in the station. Worst, as they saw the worst of people, at the worst of their times. And best, as well, they said what went, they decided how people were treated, how they were looked after, or 'looked after' in those days. I appreciate things are a lot better now, but then, well they just weren't. But Terry was one of the good ones and I think he tried to have some fun and treat people with a bit of dignity, a little respect, he was never a judge and jury type of bloke, he just did his job and kept his thoughts to himself.

T.M   Now then PC Grimes who do we have here?

PCG   He's a shoplifter Sarge

T.M   No. Who? Do we have here?

PCG.   Oh. Gary Smudgins. Shoplifter

T.M   Oh, right, sort of double barrelled then is it Gary

GS   What?

T.M   Your surname, it's double barrelled. Your parents were posh then, were they?

GS   Dunno. Never knew them

T.M   Oh. That's a bit sad. Still, let's see if we can't brighten things up a little bit. Now. Are you looking for a single, a twin or a double for tonight, Mr Smudgins?

GS   What? I'm not staying here tonight

T.M   Well, we don't rent our rooms by the hour young man, we don't run that sort of establishment here you know. No. No. It's per night or not at all

GS   Can I have no at all then mate

T.M   Oh, I like it Gary, I like it. No. And I'm not your mate by the way

GS   A single please Sergeant

T.M   Ok then, a single it is. Let's see what I have free ...no, I'll tell you what,
pick a number between one and ten

GS   Why?

T.M   Just go with it will you, lighten up a bit or we'll all be here for hours. Pick a number

GS   Three

T.M   That's more like it.

Terry turned around and pressed play on a huge tape deck that was sitting on the shelf at the back of the custody desk.

From nowhere came the sound of a band, apparently called The Clash, playing a song that just made me laugh so much. The tune was called 'Police and Thieves' and when played at full volume brought the house down.

T.M   Oh, sorry, number three is not vacant at the moment Mr Smudgins, can you pick another number

GS   Oh. OK. Five?

Again, the tape deck burst into life, this time with The Clash playing what I understand was a more popular hit of the time - 'I Fought the Law', which I thought was very funny.

T.M   Oh. Number five has just been taken I'm afraid. Once more.

GS   No. You're taking the piss now

T.M   Yes. I'm sorry. I am, I don't mean to, but it's just to lighten the mood a little, people do get a bit low when they come in here. Can I interest you in a Loyalty Card.

GS   A what?

T.M	A Loyalty Card. Look, here I'll explain. You know when you use a shop a lot, they sort of want you to come back, you know, be loyal
GS	Right
T.M	Well, I was thinking, we should do one.
GS	I'm not loyal to the police, I fucking hate the police, they keep nicking me
T.M	Yes, that's usually because you keep thieving things Gary, but just listen. You keep coming back here a lot and I thought if we did a Loyalty Card, you know as a thank you for coming here and for all the information you keep giving us, then you could earn points for being loyal. If you gave us information on say, a bank robbery, fifty points, a load of drugs, fifty points, you get the idea?
GS	Right
T.M	Then, when you've got a load of points saved up on your card, you cash them in, like your Green Shield stamps, like at shops
GS	Right…go on, I might be interested.
T.M	Then, you come in here for say murder, you cash your points in , and if you've got enough then you go out with say….I don't

know an ABH charge instead of the big
one, what do you say

GS   Yeah, I'll do that, I'll have one of them
Loyalty Cards, sounds great

T.M   Really? For fucks sake, there's one born
every day. PC Grimes, cell six, next

I had stood and listened and sniggered quietly to
Terry and all I could think of was, wasted. He
was absolutely wasted being here. He was a
thinking man doing a drudge's job, no wonder he
was longing for his retirement. I'd go mad doing
what he was doing, day in, day out.

T.M   Sorry Dorcas. Right, what was it you
wanted. Any news?

I told Terry about what I had found taped to the
underside of Baz Sturgess's desk. I told him what
it was and showed him the name and address I
had written in my little notebook.

T.M   What's all that other stuff Dorcas
D   The ramblings of a mad old lady, and a bit
of shopping I need to get later. Focus
Terry, please. What does it mean
T.M   It means that our DC Sturgess is either
running an informant that he doesn't want

the others to know about, or that, and I favour this one, he's got some dirt on the villain and he's storing it up.

D   Storing it up, storing it up for what?

T.M   I don't know, but nothing good I would have thought. Leave it with me Dorcas. This is good work. Now I must go, I hear the dulcet tones of another guest if I'm not mistaken

I also heard the screaming and shouting that was filling the custody suite outside mine and Terry's meeting place, otherwise known as Interview Room One and thought that I really must get on with some cleaning, preferably as far away from Terry's world as I could get. I really wasn't made for screaming and shouting.

A young PC then approached Terry's desk, leant over it, and quietly said

PCH   Morning Sarge, I wondered if it might be possible to speak to you privately.

T.M   Good morning PC Harris. What about?

PCH   Well, it's a private matter, so I wondered if I could talk to you privately.

T.M   That would depend on the subject matter, and whether or not the matter is so private it needs to remain so, in which case probably not, or if it's a private matter that doesn't need to be private in which case, speak publicly please

PCH It's about my condition

T.M Your condition?

PCH Yes. I have this condition, well, a number of conditions really and I rather think they're getting worse.

T.M Go on….but first a few questions

PCH Certainly

T.M Is it contagious?

PCH No

T.M Is it something that needs cream applying three times a day to somewhere only a mother should help with it.

PCH No

T.M Thank fuck for that. Is it a
     physical ailment?

PCH No, well, not really, more of a
     mental thing?

T.M Oh sweet Jesus, a police officer with a mental illness, what will they think of next? Does this mental impairment affect your ability to perform
     your duties?

PCH Definitely. Though I am trying to work through my situation by means of….

T.M   Hang on, don't go any further. You're a nutter then. You need to speak to someone I would have thought

PCH   I'm not a nutter, I think I just have a number of mental health impairments, and I'm speaking to you

T.M   Yes, agreed. But do you see these chevrons on my arms?

PCH   Yes

T.M   And do you know what they mean?

PCH   That you're a Sergeant

T.M   OK. So, you're not that mad then. You understand the basic principles of police hierarchy. And do you see what it is I am standing next to?

PCH   A desk

T.M   OK. Could you narrow it down a bit

PCH   A Custody Desk

T.M   And that would therefore make me....?

PCH   A Custody Sergeant

T.M   Well done PC Harris, you are hereby fit for duty. I am a Custody Sergeant and not a psychotherapist, and therefore I am not someone who could in any way assist you with your head.

I'm sorry, son, I'm not trying to be harsh here, but we all have our own troubles, and I am really not the person to dish out words of advice. I am sorry.

PCH   That's OK Sarge. If only the police had a department where people could speak to suitably highly trained people, confidentially, about what is troubling them, what is stopping them or hindering them from performing their duties. I think that would be a worthwhile department don't you Sarge?

T.M   FFS. You really are a nutter PC Harris, aren't you? That will never happen. Go and see FLAPS - see what she says. She's supposed to look after Personnel, isn't she?

PCH   I did go and see her. She said I couldn't 't take time off as we were short staffed and that I needed to pull myself together, either that or go and speak to someone about it

T.M   Nice. Now that I think of it, I know someone who may be able to help you. Dorcas, have you got a minute?

D   Yes Sergeant?

PCH   The cleaner?

T.M   Hey. Watch yourself son. If The Head of Personnel dishes out words of advice like that, maybe the cleaner, who knows all and sees all, may have a pearl of wisdom or two for you. What have you got to lose? Dorcas, could I ask you to have a chat with PC Harris here. Here, use the good tea. Dorcas Goode you are hereby unofficially deputised as Assistant to the Personnel Department.

And so, I made PC Harris a decent cup of tea for two and we took up positions in my office, formerly known as Interview Room One.

As the officer walked in, I saw someone who, whilst apparently young, looked so old. He had the gaunt, almost haunted face of someone so much older than his years, and who had seen some awful things and not recovered from them. He stood with the hunch of an old man and sighed like one as he sat down in the chair opposite me. He slumped at the desk between us and lay his head on his arms. His head started to rise and fall in jerky motions, and I realised he was crying.

'Now, now PC Harris, what on earth is the matter. Please don't cry', I said as I passed a hanky to him and rested my hand on his arm.

'I'm sorry, I'm sorry. I just don't know what to do' he sobbed

'Look, I'll tell you what, help me move this big old desk out of the way, clear the barrier as it were' I suggested.

We moved the desk from between us, placing it against a wall. We then put the chairs opposite, but close to each other. I put the cups of tea on the floor, and we went to sit down again. As we did, PC Harris stood crying and all I could do was reach up and put my arms around him while he wept. It seemed natural and the only thing to do, to try and ease the suffering of another human being, clearly distressed.

After a few minutes of silence, broken only by the officer's sobs and sighs he stepped back and then sat down.

D   Oh, PC Harris, whatever is the matter dear
PCH   Julian, its Julian
D   Why? What's happened to him?
PCH   No, sorry, that's my name, Julian Harris
D   Oh, right, sorry. And you can call
      me Dorcas

PCH   Hello Dorcas, how are you ?

D   Me? I'm fine. Not a lot bothers me. Let's have a chat, shall we? Whatever's the matter, Julian?

PCH   I never wanted to be a Police Officer. I never wanted to be one, my parents....they

D   They wanted you to be a police officer and you felt pressured to do what they wanted?

JH   Exactly

D   Are they still alive?

JH   Oh yes, mummy is Chair of the local Conservative Party Organising Committee for Ladies

D   Impressive

JH   And obviously you know who my father is?

D   Mr Harris senior?

JH   Yes, but you know who he is, what he does?

D   No. I'm afraid I don't Julian. I've not been living here for a long time, and I try not to read the papers, they're all just so depressing. I tend to keep myself to myself really

JH   He's the Chief Constable

D	Ah. That would be somewhat problematic for someone in your position
JH	Yes. I think he wanted me to follow on in the family tradition and follow my brothers into the Police, sort of pass it on?
D	Yes. That's not healthy, unless all parties are willing, I wouldn't have thought
JH	I was willing, I did sort of want to join the police, but I think I liked the idea of joining the police rather than actually doing it. I don't think I can do this for thirty years
D	How long have you been in the police
JH	Six months
D	Ah. Still an awfully long way to go then Julian
JH	Too far Dorcas. I'm not going to make it....and after what happened to Raymond, I don't think I should do this anymore.

'Oh? Right' I said but stopped short of asking who Raymond was and what had happened to him. Instead, I said

D	Why don't you speak to your father then? Why don't you tell him how you feel and what you fear? Could you speak to him?
JH	No. Absolutely no way

D   Why not?

JH   Have you met my father? Do you know what a tyrant he is?

D   No. I've never had the pleasure. What would you want to do, what are your dreams? If left alone, what would you do for a living, for a career?

JH   I feel like I have had no choice in any of this, like my life has been mapped out for me, like everything has been taken away from me

D   As my old mate Viktor Frankl says, 'Everything can be taken away from a man, but one thing: the last of the human freedom - to choose one's attitude in any given set of circumstances, to choose one's own way'.

JH   Goodness that's deep

D   Not really, if you break it down, it basically means you always have a choice. It may not be an easy choice and it may be a choice that has adverse consequences, but you have a choice. Do you see?

JH	I see that you're wasted as a cleaner Dorcas, ever thought if going into something else? Personnel maybe, you'd be great. Better than FLAPS, she's useless.
D	Oh, I don't think so. Why do they call her FLAPS?
JH	It's not FLAPS, like a name, we just call her that. It stands for Facilities, Logistics, and Personnel Services
D	Oh, that's good, I like that. FLAPS, I'll have to remember that. So, Julian, what are we going to do with you, eh?
JH	Oh, I'll be alright. I'll think of something to take my mind off things and stumble on for a while. Perhaps until Father retires, you know and is sitting as a CEO on some company board or other
D	Yes, but that could take years, what will you do till then?
JH	I'm going to transfer from the hustle and bustle of the streets and go into the hurly burly of teaching. I'm going to teach
D	Teach? Teach what?

JH   Policing. I'm going to go on the
              Training Department

D   But you've only been in the police for six
              months, what could you possibly teach?

JH   I have shed loads of experience Dorcas,
              and I can't wait to pass on my wealth of
              knowledge to new recruits at the
              Training School

D   ....

I was speechless.

A very strange man indeed

Because I was on my own when cleaning I had an arrangement with some offices that I would only clean as and when they thought their place needed cleaning. Some people were very private about letting what was, at the end of the day, a stranger into their workspace and would only ask me to come in perhaps once a week, I mean how much mess can they make in a day, and this suited me as it allowed me to focus on my little plan.

Some offices only really needed cleaning once or twice a week, some just needed the bins emptying, and I was particularly good at emptying bins. I understand now they have things called 'shredders' which chew up the wastepaper, the confidential wastepaper, into little strips that no one could read. Although they often show it now in films, you can't put all that mess back together and make sense of it, I don't care what anyone says.

But at the time, no 'shredders' meant good old Dorcas would take bags and bags of confidential waste out to the skips, which was then some days later taken to sites way across the country, where it was all supposedly burnt. Confidential waste my ....foot.

However, in all this cleaning there was one office that never asked me to tidy up after them, they never asked me to have a quick dust and wipe, sweep or hoover up after them, let alone tidy a wastepaper basket.   And that office was the Property Store and that made me very suspicious.

I thought I would take a wander down to the Property Store and see if I was needed and to obviously have a general nose around.

I knocked on the door and it was opened by a small man who looked like he had lived in the dark for a thousand years and was frightened of the very concept of light. He had tiny shrunken eyes and a screwed-up face like a rat. He peered at me through the thin crack between the door and frame. The hand that held the door ajar looked like it could do with a manicure once in a while, perhaps with a pair of garden shears - I thought he had claws for nails.

PO   What?

D   Hello, my name is Dorcas, I am the new cleaner. Well, when I say new, I've been here a few weeks now and I just thought I'd introduce myself and see if you needed anything

PO   Right?

D   So….I'm Dorcas

PO   Yes, you said

D   And you are…...?

PO   McAvitee?

D   Hello Mr McAvitee. That's an unusual name so far south. Please don't tell me your first name is Phil? I think I'd just about wet myself

'No. It's John' Mr McAvitee said with absolutely no humour, or perhaps no understanding, at all.

D   No. I was meaning. Phil McAvitee, like...you know, a joke type thing

JM   But it's John. John McAvitee. I'm the Property Officer

D   Oh, OK. Hello John. And what does that do then - the Property Officer?

JM   Well, I look after all the property

D   Well, that sounds very interesting. I'm a
         cleaner, well actually, I am the cleaner,
         and I look after all the cleaning. Did you
         need any?

JM   No thank you. It's all fairly clean and tidy
         here. Just the way I like it. That way you
         know where everything is

D   Oh. I do like a man who knows where
         everything is. A place for everything as
         the saying goes

JM   The saying is 'a place for everything, and
         everything in its place'

D   Quite right too. 'Place is the greatest thing
         as it contains all things'

JM   That doesn't make sense

D   It does if you're Greek - Thales of Miletus
         said it

JM   That doesn't make it right, and I'm not
         Greek, I'm from Deptford

D   No? Lots of people thought he talked
         sense though

JM   Oh, right? Who? Who thought he
         talked sense?

D   Well, I don't know exactly who, but he
         said it many years ago and people still say
         it, so it must be a bit true don't you think?

JM   I don't know. I didn't know him, I didn't hear him say it, so I wouldn't say it's true, but I suppose it does make a bit of sense, maybe?

D   There you go then, a philosophical comment that you could use here - I think Thales would be happy if he knew his words were still being used so long after his death - even it if was only as a slogan for a Property Office in Sandford

JM   He probably wouldn't know where Sandford was. Where is Miletus anyway

D   Apparently it was a Greek city on the western coast of Anatolia, which is now in Turkey. Thales was also regarded as the first to call himself a 'philosopher'

JM   Oh, really? What did they have before that then

D   Probably just old white blokes who sat about and talked a lot and occasionally made some sense to someone. But as they say 'A multitude of words is no proof of a prudent mind'

JM   Who came out with that little gem then

D   Oh that was Thales as well - talkative chap, wasn't he?

JM   I am actually quite busy. Could you come back later

D   Why don't you let me have a little dust
         and sweep and then I'll be out of your hair

Which was an unfortunate expression as, when
John McAvitee pulled the door open enough for
me to enter, I noticed he had not one strand of
hair on his very unusually shaped head.

'Do you like it down here John' I asked whilst
not quite taking her eyes off   his head.
'It's alright I suppose. I've been here for ages.
Sort of keep myself to myself. I don't bother
anyone, and no one bothers me' John said, whilst
not quite taking his eyes off me.

As I entered the Property Store which was
situated on the ground floor, though it felt
subterranean, I saw that it was a vast, almost
cavernous expanse which consisted of huge
spaces crammed full of things that people either
had found and lodged at the police station until
they were claimed; or were all the things people
did not voluntarily lodge at the police station but
which had been seized by the police as either
stolen or suspected of being stolen items.

John showed me around and was proud of his little world and his ability to organise. As we walked through his empire, strip lights came on illuminating our progress and he showed me the lost bikes, the bits of cars, the record players and the like. There were also small things like Mars bars, bags of crisps and flowers - items which had been stolen and which for some inexplicable reason had been lodged in a musty smelling ground floor store, where they invariably went mouldy in the case of the flowers or were mysteriously 'eaten by mice'. And if you believed that you were just daft, unless the 'mice' now walked on two feet and dressed in police uniforms.

We were just getting to the far end of the store when John abruptly stopped, turned around and spoke

JM   Well that's it. That's the end of the tour. I am actually quite busy.

We had stopped by a padlocked cage type enclosure, and I wondered exactly what it was that John did not want me to see, a locked door within a locked door?

The door itself was a normal door but seemed strengthened in some way, and the interior of this cage was blocked off from prying eyes by tall metal units that ran floor to ceiling.

John didn't appear to be the swiftest man in the world, and he could have steered me away from that door at any time, but it was almost like he needed to show people this, taunt them, someone, anyone, with his little bit of intrigue, his little secret. Was it to make himself seem a little bit interesting, a bit mysterious? I thought it probably was, as he didn't have too much going for him but to be honest it was a bit sad.

What I had noticed about John though, apart from his oddly shaped, totally bald head, and his talon like nails, was his jewellery. The man literally jangled as he walked. He had rings on his fingers (and probably bells on his toes), but he also had a number of gold chains around his scrawny neck and was the first man I had seen to have both of his ears pierced. Two large diamonds shone from his overly large lobes.

It may be that this was his little luxury, his way of expressing himself and spending a bit of money on things he liked, but how much did a

Property Officer earn per year. It made me think. I would speak to Terry and see his take on things.

For now, though I was spun on my heels and almost run out of this particular town. As I left, I thought I must say something to this strange little man

D   John, now we have met, and you have shown me your wonderful workspace do you think I could pop down from time to time, you know ventilate it a little?

JM   Why?

D   Well, it does seem a little fusty? A little in need of airing, don't you think? I'm saying this purely from a professional cleaner's point of view, you understand.

JM   I've never really noticed it, I can't smell anything

This did not come as a complete surprise to me having walked a thousand steps with him. Maybe it wasn't the Property Store that was a little musty, maybe it was John himself. I needed to be delicate here. I had to 'keep him sweet', I just had to see what was in his locked room.

D   No? Can't smell the overriding odour of 'closed upness'? Don't think it whiffs just a little bit John?

JM   No. Are you sure? I've been here for years, and I've never smelt anything

D   No? Well... How about one of those air freshener things, you know the ones that you stand in a corner, and it looks like a pot of flowers? Or I know, how about some potpourri ? Nice bit of
         lavender perhaps?

JM   Po what?

D   Pot pourri. It's French, although in French it actually means 'putrid pot' but that aside, it can smell wonderful, what do
         you say?

JM   Well, if it would help maybe. You do seem to know what you're talking about. Have you been a cleaner for long?

D   All my life I've been cleaning things, it's a very satisfying occupation. I dust and I sweep, I mop and scrub and all the time I'm making people's lives just a little bit better. I feel like it's God's work I do sometimes. I get to meet some really interesting people.

JM   And if, and I'm saying if, you cleaned
       down here, you'd be careful?
D   Oh yes. Definitely
JM   You wouldn't touch anything?
D   My hands would be as light as feathers on
       the breeze
JM   You wouldn't move anything?
D   Temporarily I'd probably have to, you
       know just to dust and the like?
JM   Oh yes, appreciated. But you wouldn't
       move anything permanently?
D   You mean steal something? Like what
       John? What do I need with old bikes, I
       have my own. I don't need car parts as I
       don't have a car and I think much of the
       smell is the daffs over there - who on
       earth seized them
JM   PC Grimes
D   Makes sense. Look John. I give you my
       solemn word, for I am an honest
       woman, and I promise you I will not take
       anything or move anything unnecessarily
       so help me God, or my name is not
       Dorcas Goode. How does that sound?

JM   Agreed. Dorcas, you may clean my office any time you think fit outside the hours of eight and four, other than that it's off limits. I don't like people encroaching into my work environment.

D   No, me, neither. I will respect your office times and work around them. You won't even notice me.

And so, I left the underworld and came out into the light. To be honest I did have to blink hard in the glare of the corridors. It was like I had stepped out of the darkness, and into the light - my light would come when I returned to the Property Store - but obviously not between the hours of eight and four.

Another guest for Terry, and Kangaroo Cottage

D   Hello Sergeant McDermott. May I bother you again please?

T.M   Certainly Dorcas. Give me one minute, guests arriving - you know how it is

D   Indeed

T.M   Ah. PC Grimes. We meet again. And who do we have here today?

PCG   Well thank you Sergeant. Today's contestant is Shirley, she's forty-two years old, a Scorpio and she's from Sandford. Her main interests are knitting, crocheting, and stealing just about anything that she can get stuffed up her wonderfully put together jumper

S   I did it myself. Only took me a week

T.M   Sorry love, all I heard was 'I did it'.

S   Well I did

T.M   Excellent. PC Grimes, I hope you're taking notes.

PCG   Definitely Sergeant. Shall I caution her at some stage

T.M   FFS. Has she not been cautioned when you arrested her

PCG   No Sarge, she's female, I can't
      caution her
T.M   You're a fucking idiot but I can't sack you.
      That's, you can't search her because she's
      female, you pillock.
PCG   Oh. Right. Sorry
T.M   Shirley, love, do you know why
      you're here
S   Because you're all Fascists
T.M   And?
S   Well, that's it really. You're all Fascists
T.M   Ok. Let's say that perhaps we are all
      Fascists. How does that change your
      position? How does our proclivity to lean
      towards the extreme far right in a political
      arena change your situation
S   I dunno. But you're all Fascists
T.M   Shirley. I am a very liberal man. So, I will
      say this once. You are here for a good
      reason. You still have a number of yet to
      be identified stolen items peeking out of
      your excellently put together knit one,
      pearl one cardi. You, yourself chose, in a
      country currently run by a far left
      government, to steal from your oppressed
      brothers, or sisters and then do a runner
      until, fuck knows how, you got caught by
      PC Grimes here. Is that about right love?

S Yes, I suppose so.

T.M Cell eleven please PC Grimes. Shirley, you'll be pleased to know that's all the way down there on the opposite side to the left. You could say it's on the Far Right

S Fascist !

You couldn't help but like Terry when he was on one.

==========

I was just leaving the Custody area when Terry called me back.

T.M Sorry Dorcas, could you hang about for a bit, I may have need of your…your…

D Mop?

T.M No

D Broom?

T.M No

D Sponge? What, what is it, Terry? What's the matter?

T.M There's a….guest about to arrive and they're….they're just a bit…you know….

D   No? Terry. I don't know, what is it? I've not seen you like this. This, not Terryness? Whatever's wrong?

T.M   Can you just hang about for me please?

D   Of course I will Terry, of course I will

The next guest Terry had duly arrived and was ushered in by two officers. PC Grimes was nowhere to be seen, which bearing in mind what was to happen I thought had been 'a bit of a result' as I often heard people say here.

The guest was accompanied by PC's Holden and Willis whom I had not seen before but seemed decent enough sorts, very level-headed and understanding but at the moment they seemed a little agitated.

PCH   Just shut up mate, just stop your yammering and stand there

Next guest)   You have brought the accused here for no good reason and I will ensure that they are represented properly. The process will start with me taking your names for the accused

PCW	You are the accused mate. There's no one else here except us three. Just stand there a minute with PC.......with my colleague

PC Willis then came up to speak to Terry.

T.M	Usual bollocks Steve?
PCW	Usual bollocks Sarge. Sorry. We had to bring him in, he just wouldn't stop. He's making their life a misery. We tried everything honest
T.M	That's alright mate, bring him over

The next guest whose name turned out to be Malcolm Bastwick was brought before Terry and unless you were there you wouldn't have believed it, and if you were there you wouldn't have understood it

T.M	Right officer, who do we have here
PCH	This is Malcolm Bastwick Sarge...he's....
T.M	No officer. Only answer what is asked. Are you the arresting officer?
PCH	I am Sarge, he....

T.M   Wait. And precisely…precisely mind, what has the accused been arrested for, not charged for, not sentenced for, not hung for, just arrested for.

PCH   Harassment of a tenant Sergeant

T.M   Under Section One of the Protection from Eviction Act nineteen seventy-seven I take it officer?

PCH   Yes….I…yes?

T.M   Thank you officer. Did the accused make any reply when you correctly cautioned him?

PCH   Yes Sergeant.

T.M   And what, exactly what, did he say?

PCH   I've got it written down here….I cautioned the accused and he replied "Mr Bastwick has heard what you have said officer and in the presence of his legal advisor he makes the following statement"

T.M   Oh God

PCH   "Mr Bastwick vehemently denies the offence under the Protection from Eviction Act nineteen seventy-seven and wishes it to be brought to the attention of the officer that there is no evidence of the offence for which he has been charged. Mr Bastwick was not present at the scene of the alleged offence when the alleged offence allegedly occurred. Mr Bastwick's legal advisor was however there, and he noted the following. One..." shall I go on Sarge?

T.M   Is there much more?

PCH   Loads - another two pages of my notebook, I had to keep asking him to stop or at least slow a bit so I could write it all down. I think he does it on purpose

T.M   Did he sign your notebook?

PCH   Yes Sarge, like you taught us

T.M   Good lad. Right, let's have a word with Mr Bastwick, shall we?

MB   Sergeant, I will bring Mr Bastwick before you to answer these outrageous charges. Mr Bastwick would you come here please?

At that, the only man in front of Terry spun around, stopped, and faced him again

MB   Ah, good morning, Sergeant, what can I do for you this fine morning? My legal advisor has told me that there is an issue that requires my attendance here today.

T.M   Mr Bastwick, did you hear what the officer arrested you for?

MB   My legal advisor has told me what I am charged with, yes

T.M   You are not charged with anything. You are accused of something, which following a full and thorough investigation you may or may not be charged with. Nothing has been decided yet and you will get your opportunity to tell the interviewing officers your side of events. Do you understand?

MB   May I speak with my legal advisor

T.M   Is he qualified? Legally qualified I mean. Has he passed exams and so on? Is he here, does he, in fact, exist Mr Bastwick?

MB   Obviously Sergeant, otherwise he would not be here today, would he?

T.M   I can't see him, but are you happy with his advice so far?

MB   Well, he never leaves my side and always tells me the right thing to do, so yes, of course I'm happy with his advice. If I was advising myself, it's exactly what I'd tell myself to do…legally speaking of course

T.M   Of course, Mr Bastwick. So, you are happy with the legal advice you have received and don't wish anymore. No one else here to assist you perhaps?

MB   No. Thank you Sergeant. I am happy with things so far.

T.M   Would you like a cup of decent tea?

D   Oh no Terry, no please, I've got so much cleaning to do

T.M   Mr Bastwick, this is Dorcas Goode, she is qualified to talk to people in your current situation, she has years of experience in talking to people, and I would urge you to take advantage of her services, did you want a minute with your legal advisor?

D   No Terry, please? Why? Why would you do this to me?

'It's a test Dorcas, a bit of an initiation ceremony' Terry said, with a sly smile on his face. Love him.

I couldn't really say no, and so I opened the door to Interview Room One and, feeling I ought to at least make an effort, I grabbed another chair in case Mr Bastwick's legal advisor also wanted to join us

D   Good morning, Mr Bastwick, how are you both today?

MB   I can only speak for myself, but I am fine. You will have to speak to my legal advisor when he joins us to ask him

D   Very well, did you want to wait for him?

MB   No, that's fine. I take it you are the interviewing officer

D   No, not really, well not at all really. I am just the cleaner

MB   Oh really? Then why are you not dressed like a cleaner

D   I am, I've got the mop and everything. Did you just want to chat? How's your tea by the way?

MB   It's fine, thank you. Mrs…? Miss….?

D   Goode, Ms Goode

MB   Oh, what does Ms mean?

D   It means I'm a proud, independent woman in a man's world who doesn't need the unnecessary attachment of a man

MB   Oh, you're a lesbian then?

D   No. I am not a lesbian. It's a title that describes exactly what I just said. Did you not hear me?

MB   Can I just tell you my side of things please?

D   By all means

MB	Mr Bastwick has two tenants currently residing in his property called Kangaroo Cottage, a three-bedroom property on the edge of town. The tenants are a teacher and a trainee teacher - Kerry and Emma - nice girls apparently, I've never met them.
D	Right....Kangaroo Cottage, that's genuine is it, a real place?
MB	Oh yes. He apparently built it some years ago, with money from the trust.
D	The trust?
MB	Yes. The committee that runs the trust consists of....
D	Don't tell me. Mr Bastwick, you - his legal advisor and....I'm stuck, who else....?
MB	His daughter and her daughter
D	And how old is Mr Bastwick's daughter?
MB	Twenty
D	And her daughter?
MB	Two
D	Oh, good grief - go on
MB	Mr Bastwick rented the property to the women, and they moved in. They then complained to Mr Bastwick that they didn't like the living arrangements
D	Why?

MB	Apparently, one of them wanted the larger front bedroom
D	Well, what's wrong with that, it's a three-bedroom property you said?
MB	Yes, well, perhaps I should wait for him to arrive, but Mr Bastwick's legal advisor was already residing there.
D	So....you were?
MB	No. Not me, that would be ....inappropriate

Mr Bastwick, or it could have been his legal advisor, then proceeded to tell me that despite being asked by the committee, including a two-year-old child, to vacate the property his 'legal advisor' would not. He said he had tried for some time to placate the tenants and could not understand it when they left. They had asked for their deposit back and even threatened to sue him - him!

He said that this had gone on for just over a year and that he couldn't understand what the tenant's issue was - his legal advisor seemed a reasonable enough sort of man, although he knew that some of his personal hygiene habits left a little to be desired, as he had shared a police cell with him once or twice, but that excepted, he thought he wouldn't do them any harm.....probably. I later found out that this 'once or twice' was in fact fourteen times.

Malcolm Bastwick was there, he was present in the room, but by G how I wished I was not. There was no one else in the room, but he spoke, solidly for an hour about the situation, and how his legal advisor wasn't such a bad man, and how that at one point three of the committee had actually agreed an equitable settlement with the tenants, but that they could not persuade the fourth and until she had had time to read the documentation set out before her, they really could not proceed, and so his legal advisor remained in Kangaroo Cottage and here we were….(just the two of us you understand).

I swear that happened, as true as my name is Dorcas Goode. I now wanted to cheerfully throttle Terry, but I swear that happened. It's scary that people like Malcolm Bastwick exist - they walk amongst us. They are not violent or even aggressive people unless cornered or challenged but their madness is just as damaging if you are trapped with them. I felt so sorry for the former tenants, who were not only out of a property but also down by the amount of their deposit.

I know I was, and had been, many people, but only one at a time. This poor, damaged man needed help, but being in a police cell wasn't going to help him and I doubted when he was charged that the courts would help him either. I didn't know the answer of how to help him, but I thought I might know how to help the tenants if I could find them.

The children's home

As the girl walked slowly, head bowed, hands clasped behind her, along the corridor back to her bedroom, she looked down and all she could see was the floor. Not surprising really, it was where she expected to see it, under her feet, on the floor, where it had been this time last night and the night before. If she looked up, she would have seen the sky, which again would not be unsurprising if it were not for the fact that she was indoors.

The roof on the house had seen better days, probably about a hundred years ago and had been patched in numerous places - so much so that there was more patching than the original roof, but there were vast gaps in the repairs and the wind and rain swept through them down into this particular corridor.

The floor was solid enough and had also been there where it should be, for the last hundred years or so.

The girl liked stability in her life. The roof might change, the sky might go light and dark, but the floor, well you knew where you were with a floor, solid, reliable, dependable, that's what the girl liked.

She had been sent to her room again by the Sisters. They weren't really sisters, but Sisters, and it wasn't really her room either, but a room she shared with five other girls.

She had been sent to her room this time by Sister Bernadette , who the girl quite liked and had a lot of time for. She was kind and well intentioned if a bit Goddy, but then again that shouldn't really surprise the girl as she was a nun after all, and that quality was probably necessary in her line of work.

Sister Bernadette had told the girl to lead prayers said before supper, but the girl had somehow got into a discussion about meaning and honesty

SB   Siobhan, would you please say prayers
S   I'll say a little speech of thanks, and if you
           want to call it a prayer then that's up
           to you
SB   Siobhan....just

S   Certainly Sister Bernadette, perhaps something with feeling,
something heartfelt?

SB   Yes please

S   OK then, how's this? 'For food in a world where many walk-in hunger. For faith in a world where many walk in fear; for friends in a world where many walk alone; We give you thanks'.

SB   O Lord

S   Yeah, sorry, thanks G

SB   No Siobhan, O Lord. You can't say that type of prayer

S   I can, I just have, look you've still all got your hands together and your
heads down, that's pretty prayer like

SB   No. I mean that's a Jesuit prayer, that's not the sort of prayer that we say
here. It's not the sort of thinking that we would encourage, us being Catholic
and all

S   But Sister, the Jesuits are Catholics

SB   Yes, but they're not proper Catholics

S   Not proper Catholics? What does that mean? I'm fed and watered each day by Catholic money, I sit in a Catholic church every Sunday and I dress like a nun in training. Am I not a proper Catholic?

SB   Well yes. But no. I mean I hope so, the
        Catholic bit, not the nun bit, unless of
        course… you want to be, that's a choice
        for later perhaps.

S   So If I'm not a proper Catholic why do I
        have to say a Catholic prayer, and let's not
        forget the Jesuits were a branch of the
        Catholic faith weren't they

SB   Yes, but

S   So, surely, any prayer or speech to your G
        is a good prayer isn't it, I mean if it's said
        with feeling and heartfelt emotion?

SB   Well yes. But. Why don't you say the
        word God, Siobhan. Not once have I
        heard you say the word God.

S   I have my reasons. I'd prefer to keep them
        private if that's all the same

SB   We have no secrets here, Siobhan. God
        knows all and sees all.

S   Jesus, that's creepy

SB   Siobhan ! Do not take the Lord's name
        in vain.

S   I didn't. I said his supposed son's name

SB   The Lord is God

S   So, what you're telling me is that every
        Spanish or Mexican parent who names
        their son Jesus is calling them God

SB	Well no, they are naming their sons after God
S	Then wouldn't they just call them G, not Jesus. Look I'm sorry about the speech thing shall we just eat before it all gets cold
SB	No. Siobhan. Explain your reasons why you never say the word God.
S	Because I don't believe in him. I don't believe that there is a bloke sitting around listening in to everything everyone says, and who can see everything everyone does, it's just not possible. I mean how likely is that
SB	Go to your room
S	Yep. No supper again I take it
SB	Correct.

And so, Siobhan trudged upstairs again, like she had last night, and the night before that, for, she thought, just being honest and staying true to her own beliefs.

Siobhan didn't mind living here as she felt she was only staying temporarily - it wasn't for good, it wasn't for ever, just for a little while.

She didn't mind the other residents either, they were waifs and strays just like her, and had been deposited here by a caring society, one which looked after their unwanted offspring. Instead of the regular beatings, or worse that some got at home they were lovingly dumped in a children's home run by nuns.

Siobhan did not know who her parents were as she had never met them. She had been at the home almost since birth and had never really asked that she could remember and now it didn't really matter to her anymore.

The nuns had said she could be anyone she wanted to be and had named her Siobhan, which apparently meant 'God's grace' and was originally from Ireland.
Siobhan had asked if she was originally from Ireland but had been told no. The nuns said they had a system of looking at an unnamed child in their care and just feeling what name would suit them, what God would want them to be called.

Siobhan had first displeased the nuns, when as a young child when she found a large hat in one of the offices.

The hat had bits of folded up paper in it and all she had asked was, what all the squiggles written on them meant. 'God's grace' my….foot, Siobhan now said to herself.

Since that first time she had displeased them many times, mainly through her being a questioning individual, she wanted to learn, she wanted to know why. But the nuns preferred their charges just to accept and believe and that was something that Siobhan just could not do. And as for her surname…Murphy? Strangely enough that was the name of the builders who regularly came to repair the roof, what were the chances of God's intervention in that?

So, she had been Siobhan Murphy for a while. The nuns had said she could be anyone she wanted to be and so at the first opportunity she had, she changed her name to the bland, merge into the background, name of Catherine Taylor, left the home and travelled to Nottingham to study. To learn. To ask questions and to find out why. And what better subject to do that than philosophy. Philosophy gave her the chance, for three years anyway, to ask, and ask anything she wanted.

Catherine Taylor had left Nottingham University a little richer than when she went in and perhaps a little wiser than before but with so many questions still unanswered about life. She decided that all she could do was be good, all she could do was be kind and help other people who were in need and deserved it, and who were the people who she should be kindest towards, if not the nuns. They had raised her and treated her with love and kindness, they had helped her when they didn't have to, and they had treated her like they loved her, even though she was an unbeliever and argued with them all the time.

And so, Catherine Taylor became Dorcas. Dorcas, after a woman who was an apostle of Jesus (but probably not a Spanish or Mexican one) and known for her good works and charitable deeds. Goode was well, just right, and not bad.

I am thy Lord

I went to the Custody Unit nearly every day, mainly to clean obviously, sometimes for the company, but always for the entertainment.

Many of the Custody Sergeants took their role far too seriously. Yes, it was a serious job they had to do, they had to look after people who may be guilty of some crime or other, but then again, they may be innocent is another way of looking at things.

Some of the Custody Sergeants treated arrested people as guilty from the start and dealt with them accordingly, which I didn't like and couldn't understand, and some treated those people as either stupid or like second class citizens.

But Terry McDermott was different, he really was in a league all of his own. Whilst he seemed to perform his role with care and consideration for those brought before him, he also always seemed to have a laugh and a joke with people, and I think this helped settle them down during what was naturally a stressful time in their lives.

I had just arrived and had made Terry and his colleagues a decent cup of tea when the outside door flew open. We all looked up expecting to see half a dozen coppers hanging off some hairy arsed villain still wanting to fight or see someone being rushed headlong straight down the cells in what was locally for some reason, called a crucifix run.

What we actually saw was a tall, elegant man dressed in a long white shirt, cut-off jeans and bare feet, walk unaided and confidently up to Terry's desk.

Strange man.	Good morning my son
T.M	Dad ?
SM	I am here to save you
T.M	Why thank you , though I didn't realise I needed saving
SM	We all need saving my son
T.M	You're not actually my Dad, are you?
SM	I am everyone's father, for I am thy Lord
T.M	That's where I've seen you before, I thought I recognised you

SM   I am a saver of sinners, and as every man is a sinner, I am here to save you all, for I am......

T.M   Thy Lord, yes, I get it. Look, I don't want to be rude or anything but are you alone?

SM   We are never alone my son, for my Father, and thy Father is always
with you

T.M   Shouldn't that be, 'are' - 'My Father and thy father are always with you'. I thought it was a bit crowded back here, can we have a bit of space please?

SM   No. I mean my Father, thy God, so therefore also your Father is always with you

T.M   I'm sorry, I'm a bit confused. I thought you said you were my father, and so, your father would be my grandfather. And he can't be here because I went to his funeral last year

SM   No one truly dies if they believe in me

T.M   My grandfather did, they fucking cremated him, I'd say that's fairly dead
wouldn't you?

SM   And he will sit at my Father's right hand for all eternity

T.M   I doubt that very much, he'd blow all over
        the place with just a light breeze. Look
        did you come in here with anyone or did
        you just wander in; you know for a bit of
        a laugh. We are actually quite busy so
        could we sort of move it along a bit?

SM   I am in no hurry. For as it says in
        Corinthians 8.6 'Time has only one
        Lord - God'

T.M   'But when the fullness of time had come,
        God sent forth his Son, born of woman,
        born under the law' - that's from
        Galatians 4.4. And the thing to note about
        that particular quote me old son is, if you
        are the Son of God, and you are born of
        woman, you are under the law - note
        specifically the word 'under'. And I am the
        law. PC Grimes where are you, you
        little shit?

PCG   Sorry Sarge, I waited outside - this man
        said he needed no introduction as
        everyone knew him

T.M   And indeed I do know him, for he is my
        Lord. He is also Pete Masterson and I
        presume you've nicked him for begging
        down near the market?

PCG   Exactly Sarge, how did you know that?

T.M   Because you fucking idiot, you've nicked him every day for the last week for begging down near the market.

PCG   It's an offence under the Vagrancy Act Sarge

T.M   You are an offence under the Vagrancy Act PC Grimes for standing around, doing nothing, and expecting people to pay you for it. But then again, you are an offence under the Impersonating a Police Office Act as well

PCG   I've not heard of that one Sarge, is it a new law?

T.M   Yes, PC Grimes it is - put him in cell nine, again. And if you bring him in tomorrow there will be trouble, do you understand

PCG   Who are you talking about Sarge

T.M   Mr Masterson here....where is he, PC Grimes?

D   It's alright Sergeant, he's over here. Shall I make him a cup of tea and have a chat with him for five minutes?

T.M   If you would Dorcas, we are a bit snowed under

D   Proper chat?

T.M   Yes please, keep him away from me for
       a while
D   Proper cup of tea?
T.M   Now then, steady on. Not the good stuff
D   OK. Understood
T.M   Very well. Dorcas Goode, I hereby
       deputise you as an unofficial lay visitor.
       PC Grimes if you could see your way to
       standing still just inside the door of
       Interview Room One, you may actually
       learn something.
PCG   Yes Sarge. This way please Dorcas, Mr
       Masterson....I mean....this way please

And so, I officially unofficially began a new role
in the police station, that of a newly deputised lay
visitor, whatever that was. All I knew was that
this poor man thought he was Jesus and needed
an audience. I had had a few cups of tea and chats
with some of Terry's 'clients', mostly ending in
requests for cigarettes or food, and none were
what I was looking for, but I felt this particular
client was different, or could be, with a little help.

D Hello, my name is Dorcas, here you are, have a nice cup of tea …Mr….

PM Masterson. That's the name I use here but as you know I am thy Lord. But you can call me Pete. No thanks to the tea though if it's all the same, I've been here a few times and the tea isn't really to my liking

D OK. Just a chat then?

PM Just a chat then

D What brings you here then Pete?

PM I am ashamed to say that I am accused of begging. I mean begging in the street, how low can a man get, honestly

D Oh, don't put yourself down, at least you weren't stealing or robbing anyone. You weren't breaking into someone's house, or anything were you?

PM Oh, no, I wouldn't do anything like that, I'm not a common criminal. I mean essentially, I'm just asking people for money, a bit of spare change, anything they can afford really

D Ask me

PM Sorry?

D Ask me. Ask me for a bit of spare change

PM Why?

D Just go with it, just see what happens

PM   Excuse me, you wouldn't have a bit of spare change would you madam?

D   Ooh, madam? I like that. Certainly, how much would you need?

PM   How much do I want?

D   No. How much do you need?

PM   For what?

D   To keep you out of trouble Pete, for say a month?

PM   I don't know, I've never really thought about it. I tend to live day to day. I manage to get by throughout the day, but it gets to late afternoon, early evening and I sort of run out of steam and need a hot meal and a bed for the night.

D   So you get yourself arrested on purpose?

PM   Not every day, but sometimes, when I feel a bit low, it gets very lonely and I crave the company of people, any people. They normally let me out in the mornings with a stern talking to, I mean there's no point fining me is there, I haven't got any money, which is why I beg

D   It's a vicious circle

PM   It is that

D   What would break that circle? What would help you right now? If I gave you money, what would you do with it?

PM   Probably drink it. There's no point in me having money in my hand, I'm terrible with money.

D   Do you have accommodation?

PM   A roof over my head? No. Not unless you include various bridges dotted around the city I don't

D   Right. Here is what we are going to do. I sense you need direction, a purpose in life, and I might have just the job for you, and it comes with a roof. Just a minute. PC Grimes, could I ask you to be a dear and grab me my handbag from my cleaning cupboard please?

PCG   Yes. No problem....madam

D   Thank you. Though the errand is erroneous you know

PCG   That's like urgent isn't it, I'll run both ways then

D   Bless you

PM   Steady on madam, that's my line

When PC Grimes had left his post I explained my plan to Mr Masterson, inasmuch as it pertained to him anyway. He was to attend the Police Station each day, sober, when I finished work and accompany me back to my house. There would have a hot meal and would stay on a camp bed in my garage. I would feed him and let him stay each night that he was sober. I warned him that if he ever turned up at the Police Station drunk then he would be waking up looking up at a bridge of his choice that evening. Obviously if he did not arrive as I was leaving, then I would presume he had made his own choice for the day and therefore the night. He assured me he would try his hardest to repay my trust in him.

I was trusting this man, and to be honest I didn't know why.
I had spent some time talking to him and when he stopped with the 'I am thy Lord' thing he was actually a very clever man or had been once.

Whilst he clearly had problems I didn't know if they were purely of his own making or if he had found himself in a bad set of circumstances which were out of his control and that now he could not cope with his situation.

It turned out he had been a banker in a former life many years ago in some high-flying city company, but he only alluded to the past with a sad look in his eyes and didn't want to speak any further about it.

But there was something about him that I thought I could save, resurrect from the past, something that would help him out of his current dire situation, and very selfishly, may also help me.

I had a plan of my own and felt Mr Masterson could contribute a large part to it, but first he needed to be sober, tested and trained and brought back to the world, before he would be of use to me.

Property store matters

I had been cleaning the Property Store for some weeks now. I was getting to work a little earlier than I would have liked, but it was hopefully going to be worth it. I'd 'clean' it three times a week and had established a routine of being seen getting to work early and making a bit of a fuss of having to attend to the Property Store earlier than other offices.

Anyone I saw that early in the morning, usually about seven o'clock, was either just going 'off nights' and hardly saw me or was sympathetic towards me as they came into work for 'earlies'. We had an understanding -

'blooming John the mole and his "not in my office between eight and four"'
'Tell me about it'

Everyone I saw at that time nodded in agreement, and so I was therefore invisible again, just the way I liked it. I breezed in, using my cleaners Property store key which I had been issued by John to assist him in being totally alone 'between the hours of eight and four'. I also made sure that I was seen coming out , puffing a bit as the office was 'always a mess' and 'so big' that people were getting used to seeing me that way and eventually started ignoring me. Invisible and ignored....pure bliss for me.

I had checked the main Property Store to make sure there was nothing substantial that could benefit me.

Broken bike with no chain - no
Dented rear wing of a Ford Fiesta - no.
Mouldy family pack of Rolo's -
Tempting as a snack but they seemed more in bloom than the flowers still rotting in plastic bags around the store - blooming PC Grimes.

No, I would leave all these items of temptation and focus on the locked mini store at the back of the cavern. It must contain gold and jewels; it was a grotto and there must be treasures stored within. I certainly wasn't going to entertain cleaning this weird man's Store without some reward being available to me.

I thought for days about how to get into the store and how to liberate whatever golden nuggets lay within it.

I kept coming to the conclusion that I needed keys - I know that sounds obvious but I had looked under the door, through gaps between the metal cabinets, I had even borrowed a ladder and looked from above. There was no way in, other than through the front door.

It was a frustrating problem which, I will admit, kept me awake for a few nights. I did like a challenge, and I didn't like being defeated, but this was starting to get to me. I knew if I got into the mini store at about half five I would have at least two hours a day to thoroughly search and see what was contained in all those tall cabinets - who knows I thought to myself, there may even be a safe - though that would be a problem all of its own.

On one of my almost daily visits to the Custody Unit to see Terry, I plucked up the courage to talk to him about John McAvitee and the Property Store.

I knew of no other way, and whilst it would be using Terry to some extent, and that I would hate myself for doing it, I just had to know if this was a challenge too far, or would the 'rewards justify the means', to misquote a deontological philosophy - there I told you I liked words.

D   Morning Terry, have you got a
        minute please?
T.M   Morning Dorcas, what's up?
D   Are you busy? I have a bit of a problem,
        it's a bit embarrassing really.
T.M   No. I'm not busy, I won't mention the 'Q'
        word - might be the calm before the
        storm, who knows, but how can I help
        you, so early in the morning?
D   It's just that I've left my keys at home, and
        it's seven o'clock and even if I run home
        and back again, I won't get here before
        eight and the Property Store man - that
        John feller, well he's a bit, you know,
        odd, about people not being in his office
        between eight and four
T.M   No.
D   No what. No, you can't help me. Or?

T.M   No. He's not just odd about that, he's downright fucking weird. Full stop. Here take my keys, they open most things round here, but not a word to anyone, and straight back when you've finished otherwise, I'll be whistling goodbye to my pension

D   Understood, thank you Terry, you're a lifesaver, I'll be straight back.

I went as fast as I could to the Property Store and hunted through Terry's keys as I walked. It has obviously been a lie, but he wouldn't get in trouble, and no one would need to know.

I entered the Store and locked the door behind me, double locking it so no one could easily enter after me. Most of Terry's keys were large and probably used for the cells he guarded every day. There were some which were normal door keys all labelled and the rest, of which there were many, were much smaller and unlabelled. I quickly worked through these seeing if any fit my treasure room.

I had tried about a dozen of them on the padlock when, 'Eureka!'- it opened. Why hadn't I thought of this before - a Custody Sergeant in charge of all keys to the station outside of office hours - it

130

all made sense. What didn't make sense is why when sitting in a tub of water Archimedes suddenly shouted, 'I've found it !'- it shouldn't have come as a surprise to him, surely, he was having a bath after all.

As this had all taken time, I didn't now see the point in quickly rummaging through the grotto. I didn't know what I was looking for anyway and there was no point rushing. I had to take a chance. I re-locked the cage and took the key from Terry's key ring - hopefully he would be busy when I returned them to him and wouldn't notice just one small key missing. I was putting a lot of faith in things going my way but as they say…'faith is seeing light with your heart, when all your eyes see is darkness'. I quickly made it look as though I'd been cleaning a while, locked the door and went back to the Custody Unit.

It was six o'clock in the morning, and where do you think I was at this God forsaken time of the day?
Slumbering in my nice, warm bed? Sipping a piping hot cup of tea and a bit of toast, that my husband or lover (I didn't mind which) had brought me while I slept?

Lying side by side with said husband or lover whilst we read the broadsheets and laughed at life?

No. I was on my hands and knees wading through a load of grubby old property bags within my treasure room.

Forget cups of tea and toast, this was living, this was why I was put on this earth - to make money, and then do something good with it. I had had my troubles before when it came to money and no doubt I would have trouble again, but I think I was prepared for it. I knew in my heart that whilst I did, occasionally do bad it was for the greater good, it was not for my individual benefit, but for others, and I felt that if I kept that in mind I could ease my own conscience when stealing, lying, and cheating.....oh, that sounds awful when you put them together in one sentence, but this was my life and so long as I continued to do good I did not consider myself a criminal, only someone who committed crime.

Many would say that there is no difference and that both types of people should be treated the same, but I disagree, and I have a philosophy degree on my side before anyone thinks they can argue with me. There are many great and wise people who have gone on before that would argue that it is acceptable to do some wrong if you are either doing the best for the greatest number of people, or that you are doing wrong with good intent. The problem is when you try to explain things to people who don't understand, or don't want to engage on that level. Then it seems like you're trying to teach them to suck eggs as one would say, when in fact you are just exploring thoughts, reasons, ideas and so on.

I knew I was on dangerous ground if I tried explaining my position regarding theft and fraud to the police force in the nineteen seventies. They would be likely as not, to give me a good kicking if I argued, and then just write up my admission anyway. Better I felt, to go about my business, doing what I felt I needed to do and getting out before there was any….unpleasantness.

I worked quietly and methodically through a large number of property bags within the cage. I marked in my notebook things that were of interest, things which I may be able to use, but what I was looking for was not yet to be found.
I had already looked in the tall cabinets and was not interested in what they held. There were so many guns and knives contained within them it

scared me. Someone could start a mini war if they were of a mind. I dreaded what would happen if the weapons in here got 'on the streets' as I had often heard people say. I wondered why the police just didn't destroy them all and save any issues later. I didn't know police procedures, apart from the ones I had seen and at that time didn't know they were needed as evidence against some 'villain' or other.

During my time at the police station, I had kept my ears open, and my mouth mainly shut. I obviously couldn't help but talk to people and I'd like to think that when I had cups of tea with people in my unofficial lay visitor's office, I did some good - that certainly was my intention.

Whilst cleaning the drugs Squad office I had heard the officers talking about a major seizure or 'fucking big haul' as one eloquent custodian of the law described it. This 'haul' was one of the biggest the area had known in some years, and I understood consisted of drugs, cash and what was being referred to as 'funny money'. I'd dealt a little in financial matters over the years and took this to be counterfeit cash. At that time, it was not only drugs that were flooding our streets, but it was also millions of pounds of counterfeit bank notes, and I knew that the banks had been told to take the cash in and deliver it to police stations where it would be burnt. Drugs Squad officers were apparently amazed at the size of the haul bearing in mind all the publicity there had been about it.

I knew that this 'haul' had to be in here. It had to be somewhere amongst the thousands of property bags. If I found it, I knew that I could forge ahead with my plan. My knees and back were killing me - Oh for a husband (or lover) and a bit of toast.

Every third day I got to work early and went to the Property Office and eventually I found what I was looking for. I couldn't believe my eyes. There were literally tens of thousands of counterfeit notes sitting looking at me as I walked into the cage. Someone had obviously moved them there recently as I hadn't seen them before and had been about to give up hope, but what was it that the Greek poet Theocritus said ? 'You need to have courage because tomorrow will be better. While there's life there's hope, and only the dead have none.'

I thought I had had courage and hoped that Theo would be proud of me. I hadn't given up hope....quite. I worked quickly, and when I moved the counterfeit notes, I saw an equally large bag full of cash....just lying there on the floor, one padlock protecting it from a thief ...if that thief had access to the police station and the right key obviously. My particular key was a spare I'd had cut in the next town up and not the one I'd borrowed from Terry. I had put that back when he was busy and so I now felt better about protecting him from any accusation that was bound to come. Strangely though there were no drugs to be seen. I wondered where all that had gone. I had a few suspects in mind but maybe that was a thought for another day.

My plan depended on a number of shifting factors, and blind luck was the main one of them. Looking at the two bags they seemed about the same size, and I noted that none of the contents appeared to have been counted. There were no note bands around any of the cash and the counterfeit papers were similarly stuffed into a large bag. If some of one got into the other, bit by bit, day by day who would know?

I would have to know a number of things though, like when this cash would be counted. Had anyone been arrested in relation to it, and would it ever be needed at court? At the moment I didn't know any of these things, but I felt I knew someone who may be able to find out, but it would be tricky getting such information from someone without careful planning and approach.

D   Good morning, Larry, cup of tea and a bit of toast? My treat?

LSD   Lovely, Dorcas. I could do with a break. We've been really busy

D   Oh really? Where's everyone else

LSD   Oh, when I say we've been really busy, I mean that I have. I think the DS, Baz and Vince are being busy down the cafe, or the pub, what time is it?

D   Oh it's only half nine

LSD   Pub then. They'll always find somewhere that's open, either that or knock the landlord up to inspect his licence, you know how it is.

D   Good grief, no wonder they smell like they do. Do they drive there and back, or walk ?

LSD	They really should walk both ways, but I think they spin the bottle to see who drives back
D	Spin the bottle?
LSD	Yeah, it's Baz's idea. When they think they've had enough and, Jesus, that takes time, they find a bottle and spin it on a table and if it doesn't fall off and smash all over the place, whoever catches it, drives them all back here
D	Have you ever played that Larry?
LSD	No. Whenever I'm out with them I always get nominated as…what's that term?
D	Erm….I wouldn't know….Plod?
LSD	What?
D	Plod? Is that a term, or is it plonk? I don't know, I don't know the lingo sorry
LSD	Christ Dorcas. A plod is a uniform PC, and a plonk is a female PC - a plonk or a whoopsie
D	A what? A Whoopsie? What the goodness type of sexist epithet is that?
LSD	Oh it's not sexual. Whoopsie, W.P.C. - whoopsie…although…
D	Don't got there Larry, its beneath you, you're better than that
LSD	Sorry, I got a bit side-tracked, its working with these…these

D   Neanderthals?

LSD   Exactly, Neanderthals. They are fucking animals, excuse my French Dorcas

D   Whilst I think it's not Anglo Saxon as a lot of people think, I believe the term dates from the thirteen hundred and was English in its origin. But anyway, we digress - Neanderthals, Larry - shall I get the tea and toast by the way

LSD   Yeh, that would be good Dorcas, I'm so tired I'm nearly asleep

So, I popped down to the canteen to see Ida and buy Larry and I some tea and toast. I promised Ida that I would retrieve what cutlery and crockery I could find though I told her that I was not going to empty the cups again as I felt that was way above my paygrade.

D   Here you go Larry....Larry...are you awake ?

LSD   Sorry....I think I probably nodded off. It's this drugs haul thing everyone's working on

D   And when you say everyone?

LSD   Me. I'm working on it. I am it. I am the OIC

D   Officer in charge?

LSD   Oh, I wish ! It means Officer in the Case, but OITC wouldn't scan very well so they shortened it. I wish I was in charge. Everything I do is questioned, everything I do is checked and checked again, by Baz, by Vince. The DS I don't mind, that's his job, but Baz and Vince are just...well they're just

D   Neanderthals?

       LSD I was going to say wankers, but sorry, present company and all, yes, lets say that they are Neanderthals....fucking Neanderthal wankers. Sorry. That feels so much better

D   Here to help Larry. Don't forget your tea, I've put three sugars in it - looks like you could do with the glucose.

LSD   I wouldn't care but while I'm here, slaving away like a ....well like a slave, and they're off Christ knows where bigging it up about what great Drugs Squad DC's they are - they weren't even there when it all happened

D   When what happened Larry - sorry, you have to remember I'm just a cleaner. Head down, do my job, go home, me, that's my day

And so, Larry told me of the 'big haul' - the amounts involved, the type of drugs seized and where and who from. The 'who from' was the best part for me, as far as my plan was concerned. It turned out that the whole drugs operation was being run by an outside force and that no-one in Sandford had been told about it apart from the boss, which I took to be the Chief Superintendent.

Larry told me that when the day of the planned arrests came Chief Superintendent Lard Arse had taken the day off and was playing golf with some of his pals, probably all 'masonic nonses ' according to the disgruntled DC.

When the house was raided, although apparently the correct police term now is 'visited' there was no one at home, and as the house was not currently occupied according to the local council, there was no one to arrest.

There were however three enormous holdalls sitting in an upstairs bedroom, strangely right next to an open window. If anyone had bothered to look Larry said, they would have seen a recently broken trellis leading down from the window, and, if they had followed the trail of broken trellis, it would have led to broken branches, broken fences and two trails of burnt rubber just outside the back gate.

It was at this point that Larry made a bit of an admission

LSD   I'm sorry to bang on so much Dorcas, I'm just so fed up with all this nonsense. Here I am trying to learn a trade and I have no idea what I'm doing. I haven't got a million years' service, I'm not even a Detective and yet all I hear from that lot is, 'well if you want to play with the big boys you'll have to learn quicker' and it's all so much ….

D   Nonsense

LSD   Bollocks, but yes. And again sorry. I've been thinking about my future, I really have. I think I'd prefer to be a dog handler. At least I'd be the boss and they wouldn't talk back or have a go at me all the time

D   Well. I'll get us another cup of tea and see if we can't get you to muddle through shall we. At least until you've decided what to do, career wise

LSD   Oh, it's OK. I've already decided. I've just written my CID resignation out and left it on the DS's desk. I'm f..., sorry, I'm blowed if I'm doing any more of their dirty work for them.

D   But who will carry on the investigation? Who will go after these drug people, won't they come looking for their money and drugs. Won't you get in trouble?

LSD   You are nice Dorcas, you really are, but I've got to say you're a bit naive when it comes to all of this. Have you ever been involved in any crime stuff before? Do you know anything about the criminal mind?

D   No. Not really Larry, only what I see on the tele, you know Columbus, Kayak, those sorts of things

LSD   Do you mean Columbo and Kojak?

D   I don't know, probably, it's on so late some nights I'm half asleep before the start, let alone long enough to follow the plot, but I do like that Peter Faulk, he's lovely, he is. I'd like to take him home and see what's beneath his rain mac I really would, and as for Terry Savalas's lollipop...well, look at me, I'm blushing just thinking about it

LSD   Telly

D   Yes. Telly. They're on the telly, Thursday's I think

LSD   No. It's Telly, Telly Savalas, not Terry. He's Greek you know

I hadn't the heart to tell Larry that Mr Aristotelis Savalas was actually born in New York and was about as Greek as the kebabs I occasionally treated myself to on a Friday night. I think the soon to be ex Detective had had enough of people correcting him and so I said

D   But what will happen, you know to all this, when you've gone?

LSD   I don't know. There's nothing to do really. I've done it all. There's no one to arrest, we don't know who the drugs belong to, and it would take better investigative minds than Baz and Vince to work it out. No. That cash and the drugs and the counterfeit notes will all sit in the Property Store ad infinitum as far as I see it.

D   Ad infinitum Larry?

LSD   Yeah, now that is French. I know that

Lord save us, I thought, but I said.

D   Right. Sorry, Larry, I have to go - cleaning to do and all. Please look after yourself, I do worry about you.

LSD   That's OK Dorcas. I'll be alright. I'm going to go down the pub and spin that bottle, and do you know what?

D   What's that Larry?

LSD   I'm not going to catch it. I'll be too p..., drunk to even see it

As I left the Drugs Squad office, I did feel a bit sorry for soon to be former Detective Larry Stevens-Davis. He was a nice lad, but so out of his depth. And he called me naive - what hope was there for law enforcement?

I knew now that I had a bit of time. I knew that I did not have to rush and that perhaps my plan might just work.

A plan for Pete

I had had the Lord visit me now on a number of occasions and each time he appeared to me outside the police station just as I was leaving work.

He appeared to me as the spitting image of Pete Masterson and to me, he appeared to be stone cold sober.

I got the impression from Pete that the 'I am thy Lord' version of him was fast disappearing and that hopefully, the real Pete Masterson was coming back.

I needed him fully back if he were to be part of my plan - my second plan.

We were sitting one night in my unused garage and having a cup of tea and a few toasted cheese sandwiches and I thought I needed to move things along a bit. My overall plan involved many moving parts and this one, mainly due to Pete's past ability to drink like a drowning fish, and my obsession with swapping a few real banknotes into a bag of useless counterfeit bits of paper each day I could had caused me to stall a little on this part of the overall scheme.

D   So Pete, can I call you that now, or…

PM   Yes, Dorcas, you can call me whatever you like. I am not thy Lord anymore; I don't think you are very religious anyway. Have you ever been?

D   I was brought up to be religious, I had a lot of religious people around me, but no, I have to say I questioned too much and believed very little of what I was told was 'the truth'

PM   Catholics then?

D   Exactly. But enough about me. Tell me about you. What's your story Pete? Before the 'I am your God' phase?

PM   Lord

D   Sorry?

PM   I am 'thy Lord' not 'God' - two different people, surely you know, as a lapsed Catholic, you know about the differences?

D   Ah, to be lapsed one would have to have first believed

PM   Touché

D   c'est rien, oublie ça

PM   Impressive. A cleaner who speaks French

D   Not everyone is who, or what they seem, Pete. So…what's your story

PM   A fact for a fact, what do you say, sort of pass the time. But it has to be the truth, an actual fact, no lies, are we agreed?

D   Yes. Alright. Fact, I was brought up in a Catholic children's home having been abandoned there

PM   Fact. I was once a city banker who owned three houses, a yacht and played golf with all the top dogs in town

D   Fact. I have a friend who works in a bank

PM   Fact. Not that interesting....unless?

D   Unless?

PM   Unless you want to work in a bank?

D   Not a fact

PM   Or use someone who works in a bank?

D   Potentially a fact Pete...go on

PM   I had it all. I had all the trappings that go with being someone. I thought I was made for life and then, bang, it all went. It all just blew up in my face

D   Why? How? What on earth happened. And remember you have to tell me the truth

PM   I worked hard every day, went away a lot, was never at home, any of my homes really. I 'played away' as the saying goes

D   'Played away', I'm sorry, I don't know what that means

PM	I had affairs, I slept with women other than my wife. I was unfaithful
D	Oh
PM	I shagged around
D	Yes. yes. I get it, I'd just never heard the expression before. And a lot of people do you know, 'play away' - it often leads to problems though. So, what happened?
PM	Well, while I was 'playing away', so was my wife, with my best mate, a bloke called Marcus, Marcus Llewellyn, stuck up, poncy name, eh?
D	Names are not for me to judge. Just as an aside though, what was the name of the woman, or women you were seeing whilst your wife was seeing Mr Llewellyn
PM	It doesn't matter
D	It does. I'm interested
PM	Shoo Shoo
D	What? What's a Shoo Shoo
PM	She was
D	She was what?
PM	That was her name. Shoo Shoo, I never knew her surname
D	Oh Pete, I'm sort of getting a feeling that your wife seeing our Marcus for a protracted period of time, and you seeing

Shoo Shoo and others probably with similar names, are two entirely different things?

PM   Don't judge me, I was off my face most of the time. I had so much pressure on me I needed an outlet and so, like so many before me I went with drugs, alcohol, and call girls. I'm not proud of it. I lost everything

D   I'm so sorry, what happened

PM   My wife left me

D   She found out about the call girls?

PM   In a manner of speaking she did. As I say I was using so many drugs then, just to keep going, to keep the money coming in for the bank, that I forgot who was where and said to my wife that I'd meet her at our place in the South of France - sort of a getaway for a few days sort of thing?

D   So? I don't see a problem there

PM   No? Apart from when we got there Shoo Shoo and three of her friends were already there, having a party, waiting for me, naked and swimming in our pool

D   Ah

PM   Indeed

D   And so she left you.

PM   Yes. Divorced me, told the bank all about the things I'd done. I was so up to my neck in debt that what she didn't take, the bank took back from me in lost revenue and to settle loans I'd taken out with them….

D   For the drugs and girls

PM   Yes, for the drugs and the girls

D   Goodness Pete, that's sad. Fact. I'm going to offer you a way for you to get back on your feet. Properly, a steady income and everything. Interested?

PM   Why? Why would you offer me that….and don't lie, you have to tell me the truth

I had spoken to many people referred to me by Terry and like-minded Custody Sergeants over the last few months. I had been looking for the right person, to change, to help….no, to use. If they were helped whilst helping me, then so be it, everyone would be happy, everyone would win, and Pete was that person.

And so, I laid out my second plan to Pete. I didn't tell him about what I was doing at the police station with the notes and counterfeit paper, that might come later, but I told him that everything I was doing now was for the greater good, for others and not for my personal wealth or well-being. I told him that if he helped me, he personally would be wealthy again and back on his feet. Maybe he wouldn't own three houses and a yacht, but he would be comfortable.

Pete agreed and promised to stay sober and daily I set him tasks. In the beginning it was like training a small child. I would ask him to go to a shop with my money and come back, with a small item and the right change.

As the days and weeks went by the amount of money, I gave him grew larger until one day I asked him if he would like a bank account, into which I would place some money for him to start fending for himself.

He was hesitant at first but started to come around to the idea. I think he quite enjoyed the stability of my garage in the evenings, our chats and so on, though I did not know what he did during the day.

Casually one day, I asked him if he still enjoyed golf, to which he said he did but that he didn't have any clubs of his own and was very rusty, having not played since he used to belong to a club in Ireland, or was it Portugal - oh how the other half must have lived, though they probably couldn't remember it.

One evening I advanced my second plan a little by giving Pete a set of golf clubs and enough money to go to the local driving range for a bit of practice.

He was so overwhelmed he wept in my arms. These men, weeping in my arms, it was becoming a bit of a habit and it unsettled me somewhat. I needed strong people around me; Pete would have to toughen up if he was to be of use to me.

Over the next few weeks, I continued to swap the bank notes and counterfeit paper over in their bags and still could not believe that no one had moved either to a safer place other than lying on a storeroom floor. The holdalls obviously belied their content, but if people only knew or bothered to read the attached labels they would be as stunned as I was.

Over these weeks Pete had progressed with his golf and had opened a bank account at the bank where my 'friend' Trevor worked. I topped the account up as and when needed and was pleased to see quite a balance developing.

Pete obviously took a little out now and again, but always asked me if it was alright.

A breakthrough point in our relationship came one evening as we sat on camp chairs in my garage and ate our toasties and drank our tea. I would not let Pete into my house, and he had not mentioned alcohol for some time and so I thought it best not to upset the status quo of our arrangement, which he seemed happy with.

PM   I need to ask you a question. And please answer honestly

D   Of course Pete, what is it, has something happened?

PM   I've been asked to play golf at the local club

D   That's wonderful Pete, really wonderful. So, what's the problem?

PM   It's the way I look really. Overall, I mean. I know I dress down, as you like me to, when I'm walking about during the day, and that's OK, it really is. You've helped me so much, but I'm embarrassed to ask you for more

D   Pete. One day I will ask you to help me and I'm hoping you will. What is it? What do you need?

PM   A suit. I need a suit. One that a banker would wear

D   Is that it? A suit?

PM   Yes. Is it too much? Just tell me, and I'll make do with sports jacket and slacks, it's no bother, it's just that…

D   It's just that what Pete, please tell me, the suspense is killing me

PM   I've met someone

D   Oh? Are they nice?

PM   Erm…yes, they are, I suppose

D   Do you like them?

PM   Well, yes, in a way

D   And do they like you?

PM   Yes, I suppose so. We've been talking for a few weeks now, and ….hang on, what are you thinking?

D   A lady. You've met a lady and you want to look smart for her, maybe impress her with a sharp suit?

PM   No….no….nothing like that. It's a bloke actually

D   Oh. Right….I knew I'd asked you to change your life around, but not that far…what would Jesus do Pete, have
a word !

PM   No Dorcas, not in that way, let me finish
      for goodness sake or this could go
      horribly wrong

And so, Pete told me that he had been going to
the driving range a few times a week and that was
where he had met someone, a man, just another
aspiring Jack Nicklaus or Gary Player, whoever
they were, and that they had asked him to come
to their club and have a round of golf with him
and his friends.
I told Pete that I thought this was a great idea,
and that it would help him get out and about,
meet new people and get his old confidence back.
I told him I couldn't be happier for him.

D   That's brilliant Pete, and has this person
      got a name?
PM   Colin.   Colin   Bradley,   Bradman,
      something like that?
D   Bradshaw perhaps?
PM   Could be, why? Do you know him, seems
      a decent chap, funny handshake though,
      bit too touchy feely for me, but
      alright really
D   And what does Colin do for a living Pete?

PM   Oh he says he's a civil servant. I don't
     know probably only works for the
     Council or something

D   And what did you tell him you did?

PM   Well, that's the reason for the suit really. I
     told him I worked for a bank in the city,
     so I need to look the part.

D   Oh right. And how do you feel about not
     telling the truth

PM   Well it sort of is true, but it sort of isn't, if
     you know what I mean?

D   Pete. It's sort of an absolute lie if you
     know what I mean

PM   Yeh, OK, I know, but it's an in Dorcas,
     an in

D   Oh more than you know Pete, more than
     you know.

I then told Pete that I was happy to buy him a suit
and that I hoped his game of golf went well. I
had in mind a little light following and said I
might pop up and have a bite to eat at the club on
the day, if that was in order, which Pete said was
no problem. I told Pete not to acknowledge me in
any way, and that he probably wouldn't recognise
me in any event.

A round of golf, a funny handshake, and a surprised panda

It was Pete's big day and as it turned out I had taken a day off work. I'd said that I wasn't feeling well and that I'd make it up tomorrow. No one really seemed to care, and no one asked me what the matter was, it was like I was unimportant, as well as invisible and ignored - brilliant !

Pete knocked on my door quite early in the morning. His round of golf was set for just after lunch, at eight minutes past two - why so strangely timed I didn't know, but Pete told me that's just the way golf was and so I didn't query it further.

I'd purchased Pete a sharp suit, as he'd asked, and he looked very natty in it I had to say. His cover story was that he'd taken the afternoon off to play and that a light lunch would be just the thing before a relaxing game in the afternoon, but that he had to come straight from work with his clubs, and that he'd left the bank to his staff for the rest of the day.

If anyone asked, he had a great cover story all prepared, which we had rehearsed the night before. Pete had been working in the overseas branch of an international bank and had been called to the UK to resolve some minor issue or other. He wouldn't be staying long, perhaps a few months or so and as he didn't know many people in the area and so he was looking for a few like-minded individuals to pass some time with until he went back overseas. Hopefully this would help him blend with the others at this overly posh setting.

We called a taxi at about eleven o'clock and made our way to the club. I jumped out about half a mile away and told Pete I would see him at home later on, and to remember not to acknowledge me in any way if he saw me. If I was spotted by Chief Superintendent Bradshaw all our....my, plans may very well go astray. I had the feeling that Lard Arse had not been a proper copper for some considerable time, but even so, he may suspect something.

I'd donned some heavy make-up and wore a tight scarf over my head to prevent people from seeing too much of me. If challenged I knew I also had a cover story ready, but I needed to get close enough to see and hear what Pete was saying and what he could find out.

I'd been in some similar situations before, pretending to be someone I was not, and it was quite exciting but nervy thinking what we could glean from this day, but also what could be lost if we were 'rumbled'.

I walked up to the club and went to the bar. Asking for a gin and tonic I sat down and looked around. I could not see Pete, but I could hear him expounding on modern day banking techniques and how they had changed over the years. It sounded mind numbingly boring, but the chinless wonders surrounding him seemed to be lapping it up and asking all sorts of questions. Pete was doing very well deflecting too many personal questions and focussed on the bank, the bank, the bank - its profits, and what was good and what was not at the moment, investment wise. I had no idea what he was on about, but people were actually taking notes. There really are some born every day aren't there?

Whilst I was pretending to read a bar menu but still looking around, my eyes caught the supposed Council employee waltz into the club. He was alone, but the moment he walked in he was surrounded by the people Pete had been talking to and I wondered, why so quickly? Pete had had these people almost eating out of the palm of his hand until Colin 'Lard Arse' Bradshaw had entered the building.

Each of the sycophants shook Bradshaw's hand warmly and made such eye contact with him I thought they were having a staring contest. Eventually Pete was introduced to Bradshaw by the chinless wonders, at which everyone laughed, and I heard Pete explain that they already knew each other and had done so for a few weeks.

The group moved towards the bar and so I took my G and T to a table a short distance away. As I did another person walked into the room and went immediately to Bradshaw and shook his hand. Again, the eye contact was too deep and way too long for two men, for my liking, and I swear I saw one almost bow to the other. The new man to the group leant into Bradshaw's ear and said something I could not hear but at which he nodded and shooed the other man away.

The new man stood apart from the group and as he turned towards me, I recognised him, though I don't think he recognised me.

He started to walk towards me and as I tried to get up and move to another table my path was blocked by a pair of far too tight orange trousers and what I thought could only be a cucumber rammed down his trousers.

Strange man (SM)   Hello sweetheart, all on your own?

D   It would appear that way, you are very perceptive

SM   Want a bit of company, or are you waiting for someone?

D   No. I'm here all by myself, trying to have a quiet drink and a quick bite to eat. How long does a round of golf take, do you know?

SM   About four hours

D   Really? Goodness, well may be a slow bit of lunch then

SM   So, would you like some company then? I'm here for a while as well

D   Your country is a free country, so if you must sit at a table, please sit, though I'd prefer you sit a little further away from me. You are currently blocking my view

SM   Yes. But do you like what you see?

D   I can't 'see' anything, and to be honest young man, I doubt all of that is yours

SM   You don't know that it could be.

D   I seriously doubt it. Look. Sit down if you are going to, but for goodness sake, sit opposite me, your Old Spice is making me rather nauseous

SM   It's Brut actually. You don't like it? My name's Barry by the way, what's yours?

D   It's Nadia, and mine is a gin and tonic, if we're going to be here for a while

BS   Oh? OK then. An older lady who knows what she wants. I like that

NT   And I would like a gin and tonic before the bar shuts. Don't be long

I had no other option. Honestly. I had recognised DC Baz Sturgess as soon as he turned to face me but even though he stared fully at me he was either blinded by my obvious beauty, or perhaps by my dazzling portrayal of a Russian heiress fallen on hard times. Either that or he was already drunk.

This fine specimen of manhood returned from the bar and said he had to briefly visit the powder room, but that he would be back very soon. I thought that was a strange expression for a grown man to use - more of a lady's saying - I thought men said things like 'I've gotta go and syphon the

python', or 'I've gotta go and spray the roses' and if their visit was potentially longer, the wonderful admission that they were a family man and that they 'had to drop the kids off at the pool'.
Powder room?

My gin and tonic and a pint of bitter were placed on my table by a lanky, spotty youth with a high-pitched voice and a far too tight waistcoat, who asked me if it was on the gentleman's tab, to which I replied in the affirmative. I could hold my drink and thought someone else may as well pay if I was here for a while. You wouldn't expect a Russian heiress to degrade herself with dealing with money now, would you?

Barry returned and seemed very buzzy, very agitated, but in an excited way.

NT	Are you alright young man? You seem different to when you…left?
BS	Don't worry about me darling, I'm fine, I'm buzzing I am. I'm all good
NT	And are you aware of what's going on at the moment?
BS	Yeah, of course, what do you mean?

NT   Your English drink has arrived, perhaps you can erase your white moustache off with the dark fluid when you drink it

BS   White moustache, what are you on about ?

And as Barry touched his upper lip, he quickly wiped away whatever was there, and looked around towards the bar and in particular at Bradshaw.

BS   You mustn't say anything, right? Promise me you won't say anything?

NT   I won't. About what?

BS   Did you want some?

NT   Some what? I don't know what you're talking about

BS   Some Charlie? Some blow? Some dust? Some nose candy?

NT   Young man. You really are not making sense

BS   Some Brazilian marching powder?

NT   No? Still not with you. Look, I think it's time for you to go, don't you?

BS   For fucks sake woman, did you want some cocaine or not?

NT   Not. Now, you are going to stand up, smile sweetly and walk away

BS Oh yeah. Or what?

NT Otherwise my friends over there, Sergei and Vladimir, are going to come over and speak to you in Russian words of one syllable which all mean 'fuck off', and this will be your opportunity to disappear. If you do not do it voluntarily, you will do so, Russian style

I loosely pointed over to two large, well-built gentlemen who were standing drinking water and wearing identical suits. They seemed like they were guarding someone, or waiting for someone, but it wasn't me.

Barry started to get up, looking a little shaken and a little bewildered as to where to go, and I couldn't help it, and so I said

NT Oh, and take that cucumber out of your trousers, it looks ridiculous

BS It's a courgette actually

NT Yes? That figures…Sergei? Vladimir?

BS I'm going, I'm going, fucking Russians. They get everywhere

NT They will one day

I now sat on my own and looked around. Pete and his new friends had gone into the restaurant area, and I couldn't follow as I was not a member, or a guest, so I decided I would wait a little and see if he came back my way, with any update before venturing out to the course.

Honestly, grown men chasing a little ball around a field for four hours, whatever next? I mean what was the point.

About an hour later Pete walked through the bar and towards the toilets

D   Psst
PM   No. I don't drink any more, you know that. Any way I don't know you, don't talk to me
D   No. Psst, not pissed, Pete
PM   I know, I was joking
D   I'm too tense to joke. How's it going?
PM   Yeah, not too bad. They all seem alright. The group I'm playing with has a bloke with such a small handicap it's untrue
D   Oh? That's sad, though you shouldn't say things like that, I think the new term is disabled. What sort of handicap?
PM   I don't know yet. A small one though. He keeps saying he has a small handicap

D	Maybe he just has a limp or something?
PM	What?
D	Or one leg longer than the other?
PM	What? That would be a big handicap, especially in golf, you'd be leaning all over the place, your hook might straighten out though
D	Oh goodness, a man with a hooked hand, how did he lose it?
PM	Lose what?
D	His hand. You said he had a hook
PM	No. A hook. A hook. The opposite of a slice?
D	A slice of what? Pete, I've no idea what you're talking about. Oh, look out, here comes Lard Arse
PM	Who?
D	Now he's got a large handicap I bet, but I don't know what it is just yet
PM	Oh no, he plays off a ten, that really quite small
D	No I mean he's a rude, arrogant Lard Arse, that's his handicap. Look Pete, please, don't talk to me anymore. Go to the loo and don't talk to me anymore, just till we get home.

At that Bradshaw brushed past me and patted Pete on the shoulder on his way to the toilet. He signalled to Barry who was propping up the bar, and like a puppy he practically chased his boss into the toilet. Funny handshakes, starey eyes, Lord help us, just what sort of club was this?

A couple of minutes later, Bradshaw and Barry came out of the toilet, surely too soon for a syphon draining and definitely too soon for a pool visit with the kids. The two of them walked back across the bar where Barry took up his place as Bradshaw continued to the restaurant.

Pete then came out of the toilet and as he walked past my table, expertly ignoring me, he dropped a little clear plastic bag on my table and without stopping waved to Bradshaw and re-joined the group to have lunch.

I had no experience of drugs at all, but I had watched enough police shows on tele to know that this was a 'deal bag' as they said in the trade. It had a little sticker on it which looked like a panda, though this panda looked so surprised it was as if someone had snuck up behind it and shouted 'boo' right in its ear, or worse - I don't know what drug people do with pandas, or why they are used as symbols - I blame the WWF myself.

I pocketed the bag and waited another hour. The same little scene played out almost on the hour and another surprised panda deal bag was dropped on my table as Pete returned from following the two police officers to the toilet. I know that sounds bad, but just keep thinking 'doing God's work, doing God's work' and it won't seem as suspect as it sounds.

I saw that Pete and his group had finished lunch and having been given a thumbs up from him as he made his way out to the course, I thought there was no point me sticking around any longer and called myself a taxi back home.

Tea and a cheese toastie - I thought after all this excitement. For once in my life, I couldn't wait to go to work in the morning. I had business to attend to, and it was more than just cleaning. Things were coming together.

A problem for Trevor

It was Sunday, I had a day off and I intended to use it wisely. I had awoken early as I often did and as I slumbered in my double bed - minus the husband (or lover) but with tea and toast I mulled over how things were going.

I had a three evenings a week job in the bank that was going well but my plan for that needed to be advanced.

I had a five day a week job at the police station, which was supposedly just mornings, if I was quick, but those mornings had to start at six o'clock at the latest if I wanted to get everything done cleaning wise, let alone any other business I was trying to resolve around my actual paid work.

My counterfeit note / cash swapping scheme was going well and as far as I could see no one had yet come for the bags, or even moved them. I had lightly marked the floor where the bags were when I first saw them, and they had not been moved for some months. I thought I needed just a little more time to swap all of one into the other, but then I had to formulate a plan as to how to get the actual cash out of the station.

I had found, with Pete Masterson's help that Baz Sturgess was corrupt, though I sort of suspected that from the start - he did very little police work that I could see and was always on the phone and then 'popping out to see a snout', or 'a man about a dog'. I personally thought these were euphemisms for supplying drugs, as Pete has seen him do to Lard Arse Bradshaw, but how to prove it?

As it turned out Terry was way ahead of me in that regard, though I didn't know that at the time.

Whilst checking on what I now thought as my cash, not personally mine, but for my purposes, I had seen one of the tall cabinet doors open and saw inside that a few of the larger guns had gone. This worried me as, firstly, they were guns, secondly, they should not be gone, they should have been destroyed or at least secured properly, and thirdly, if they had gone, I didn't know where, and who had taken them, or was that fourthly?

Again, unbeknown to me, Terry was way ahead regarding the guns.

He really was a busy man, that Terry, but I had only ever seen him behind that Custody Desk, working away, being pleasant to the 'clients' he saw. I've no idea how he had any time for anything else. He'd told me he used to be a Detective but that due to 'artistic differences' with those above him he had found himself 'moved for his career progression' to the Custody Unit. Maybe Terry was using his old skills trying to make one last splash before he retired.

My musings were shattered by a loud knocking on my front door.
I hoped it was not the police, coming to arrest me, having found out about my little plan.
I hoped it was not Pete, gone back to his old ways - that really would scupper things for me.
I also hoped it wasn't a bunch of Jehovah's Witnesses, I wasn't in the mood - although often I did discuss things with them, and usually I timed them to see how long it took them to walk away from my front door - my record so far was
seven minutes.

I quickly threw on a dressing gown and went downstairs. When I opened the door, I found it was Trevor from the bank.

D	Morning Trevor, goodness me, whatever's the matter? Whatever has happened?
T	Can I come in please Dorcas? I need to talk to you. I need your help
D	Of course, of course Trevor, come in. Please sit down. Would you like a cuppa?
T	Thanks Dorcas. I'm sorry to just come round so early - I didn't interrupt anything did I ?
D	No. No. I was just thinking to myself whilst having a bit of toast - want some?
T	No. I'm good, thanks
D	So, Trevor. How can I help?
T	It's a bit embarrassing really. I know we've always been able to talk but I need to offload to someone, and I can't talk to anyone at work, I can't, I really can't - no one would understand.
D	Trevor, this sounds serious, whatever has happened. Have you done something wrong
T	NPA's
D	NPA's? I don't know what NPA's are, Trevor, what do they do
T	Nothing. That's the point, well sort of
D	And who do they belong to?

T No-one. That's the point as well. NPA's means Non-Personal Accounts -
they are a way that the bank balances things. You know all sorts of things

D Not really. But what you're saying is there are these things that don't do anything, don't belong to anyone and you're embarrassed about them Trevor, I think you better explain to me what's happened.

Trevor then told me things that perhaps he shouldn't have done, but at the end I was glad I had just made a big pot of tea, as he needed it, and I needed him to keep talking.

Trevor said that Non-Personal Accounts, or NPA's, were the bank's accounts, a way of sort of storing things that couldn't go anywhere else. They didn't belong to customers but were used to lodge money for all sorts of reasons whilst different transactions went through and then they were all balanced twice a year and should all come back to nought.

They were similar for example to a solicitor who would have a 'clients account' say, for the sale of a house. The client would sell their house and the solicitor would lodge the proceeds into the clients account, and then when the client needed the money to purchase their new house the solicitor would transfer the money out to them, bringing the clients account down to zero.

Trevor said there were loads of these NPA's within the bank, to assist them in moving things around for people without them putting it in a particular person's account or profiting from things that were not theirs.

I've said before and I'll say it again, I don't consider myself a criminal, but goodness me, I do have a criminal mind. Trevor explained in more and more detail and then told me that to share the workload, a member of staff was chosen each six months to balance the NPA's and that this time it was his turn.

He told me that they were in an absolute mess and that he had no idea how to balance them and it was just embarrassing for him. Trevor had been at the bank for some years and had always managed to avoid taking his turn; he had always taken the last week in May and November off as holiday, just to avoid having to deal with the NPA's.

He said that they terrified him, but that he had no more annual leave left, and he had already been told that it was his turn.

D   I may know someone who could help you, though it would come at a cost Trevor - sort of I'll help you, you help me?

T   Anything Dorcas, anything, I don't know who else to turn to. What have you got in mind?

D   Let me deal with that. What I need you to do is bring all the paperwork home and let me look at it. Is it on one of those computer things, can it be printed off or is it in good old-fashioned paper already.

T   Paper. There is one other thing though, something I'm not going to be able to resolve.

D   Go on.

T   I've sort of been borrowing some

D   Some?

T   Some money, just a little, a little from each account. But it all stacks up you know. It's never going to balance. It's like a juggling rice

D   Oh, that's a good analogy - I've not heard of that before. How much have you....borrowed Trevor

T	About ten thousand
D	Ten thousand pounds?
T	About

I then told Trevor to do as I asked and bring the paperwork here, to my house.

A few hours later Trevor returned, and by that time Pete had washed and dressed and I had cooked him a hearty breakfast - he was going to need it if he was to help Trevor. What a pair of bankers they were !

I left them to sort things out as best they could and went out for a walk. I didn't know where I was going but I needed to think, to think how I could use this new situation at the bank for my own devices, to further my plan for the future.

I returned just as it was dropping dark and found Trevor and Pete swamped with bits of paper, but they seemed in good spirits.

D	What's going on then chaps? All sorted?
P	Nearly. We're down to the last few but we're getting there, aren't we Trev?
T	Ye ah, we are Pete, thanks again for your help, it doesn't seem so bad now it's all laid out. We are allowed to bring it all

home, but my wife would kill me if I brought all this to ours, and my kids would probably just draw all over it - chaos, it would be, absolute chaos !

D   So it all balances then? How can it?

P   Well, that's the thing. We're happy we know that most of them balance, but one doesn't

D   How much by?

P   It's not as bad as we first thought - it's not ten thousand pounds

T   No, it's only seven and a half

D   Oh ! That's OK then isn't it, just seven and a half….so what do we do?

Pete then explained that….well, let's just say that due to his past experiences he had often had to 'move things around a bit' and make it seem all was good, when in fact it wasn't. He admitted that whilst it all looked good on the surface, things under the water were normally far from good and that when the plug was pulled it usually ended with someone losing everything - being divorced and losing three houses and a yacht in his case.

But Pete seemed confident that things could be covered up, in this case, if not forever then certainly for a while and that time might give Trevor a chance to pay things back……but only if he had about five years, which is what he would get if he was discovered.

Pete and Trevor put it all back together and that is when I offered to help. I said I had some spare cash and that I was happy to lend it to the pot provided I got it back at some stage. If my money could be worked into the mix, then would this help, I asked.

As you know I've had grown men hug me and weep on my shoulders, but two at the same time is a first, even for me. When they had calmed down a bit I went and got my cheque book.

Pete reminded me that it couldn't be a traceable cheque that was paid in to the NPA's and that it had to be cash, but I was way ahead of him. I got my hat and coat and told them I would be back in a little while, telling them that I knew people who knew people. When I returned, I plonked seven and a half thousand pounds in very used, very worn notes on the kitchen table.

Trevor asked me a question that I would have preferred he hadn't, and so I didn't answer him. All I did tell him was that the money may be eventually missed but that it would do for the time being to resolve his issue and probably keep him out of prison. He said he would do anything for me, absolutely anything, and he knew that the time would come when that favour would be cashed in, so to speak.

Trevor left and I sat a while with Pete, having yet another cup of tea and this time I let him stay in the house. The nights were drawing in and the garage was no place for a grown man to sleep in the winter. Pete stayed in the guest room and couldn't be happier.

We agreed that our plan needed to move a bit quicker and so we both needed to speak to Terry. Pete had been working for Terry in a sort of 'drunk man surveillance' way around the town and so far, Lard Arse Bradshaw hadn't spotted him, after all he was perhaps looking for the sharp suited man who had beaten him so easily at golf, and that man would never be found.

FLAPS down

I had been at the police station for some time and apparently, I was due what was now called a 'review' or 'appraisal', but I didn't understand is how I could be appraised if no one saw me or even knew exactly what I did. I was just the cleaner, but apparently as I was staff, I had to have one. Secretaries had one and all they did was type, I was told, I was no different I was told, and although I could type I thought it better not to argue the point that there was a lot of difference between the two roles. And so, I went to see FLAPS…sorry Suzannah, with a z and an h don't forget.

I knocked on her door and waited….nothing, and as the door was locked, I couldn't just breeze in. I could hear voices within the office and so I thought I had the time wrong. Suzannah had said ten o'clock and it was now five to. Perhaps if I waited five minutes to see if she came out.

I heard the voices continue in the office and at one point I thought she was in distress, perhaps being attacked by the other person in there. Honestly. The noises I heard sounded like either she was being attacked, or the person with her was something akin to a wild boar.

I made up my mind, she was in danger, she was my boss, and while I didn't really like her, I couldn't let her be attacked by some wild animal….in broad daylight. And so, I shoulder charged the door….

There are lost tribes in Africa who, I've heard have strange rituals when it comes to repentance and regret. One of these tribes is said to encourage their people to pluck their own eyeballs out if they look upon a priest, or a woman who is not their own wife.

When I was outside FLAPS' door I had both eyeballs, I could see perfectly. When I shoulder charged the door, I had a clear sight of the door coming so fast up to my side, but it was only when I went through the door that I wished I belonged to that tribe in Africa.

What I saw was not a priest, it was not some idol I must not gaze on…no, it was worse, so much worse than that. What I saw was Suzannah, with a z and with an h, half naked and being held over one of her lounging settees, not by a wild boar, but by a man, similarly attired, whose face I could not see, but whose flabby white….let's say posterior I could clearly see as he stood
behind her.

Trying not to throw up I said

'I take it this is a bad time for my appraisal Suzannah, shall I come back later?'

And to her ultimate credit Suzannah calmly said.

'It's not that time already is it, Dorcas? Perhaps can we push it back till eleven? Would that
be convenient?'

I turned on my heel and thought, a little dusting in the Custody Unit would be in order.

D   Certainly. See you then Suzannah.
      Good day Detective Sergeant Fairbourn

DSF   Dora

And with that I left, trying not to run down the corridor.

I returned to Suzannah's office an hour later and knocked, and this time I waited until she came to the door and opened it. I must admit I did flinch when she bid me enter and after I had found a proper office chair in another office I sat in front of her desk

SD   So Dorcas

D   Suzannah

SD   We meet again

D   Indeed. We meet again......review then

SD   Yes. Review. You've done so well this year, you really have. I can't find a bad word to say about you or your work

D   No. Best you don't. I think I've sort of got you over a....barrel? Is that the expression?

SD   Can we at least be professional about this Dorcas

D   Oh yes, Suzannah. We can be professional, no problem, probably about as professional as shagging DS Fairbourn in your office in broad daylight

SD   Frank and I are in love

D   That's nice. What do we do then, this
         appraisal thing then.

SD   Right. So, I will go through the form and
         let you know what I've written about you
         and your work and so on. Then we discuss
         it, I write my little piece and then you can
         have your say.

D   Oh. OK. Off you go then.

And Suzannah began to go through my appraisal.
It was strange being so described and I did feel a
lot of it was copied from other people's reviews,
what I think is now called 'cut and pasted' but it
all sounded so pompous, so 'job speak' as Mr
Orwell had once said

Technical Ability - Dorcas shows an innate
                    ability   to   handle   the
                    minimum tools of her trade
                    to maximum efficiency

Communication -   Dorcas has excellent
                    communication skills,
                    knowing when to talk and
                    when to keep absolutely
                    silent and listen to those
                    around her

Teamwork -   Whilst for the majority of
                        time Dorcas works alone,
                        she has shown excellent
                        team skills and should be
                        commended   for   her
                        willingness to learn and
                        take from others

Commercial - Dorcas understands the needs and
Awareness   objectives of the modern-
                        day   police   organisation   and
                        constantly strives to achieve those
                        ends, whilst maintaining focus and
                        dedication to her individual role

Accountability - Dorcas takes ownership of her
                        deliverables and admits
                        her mistakes

Collaboration- Dorcas demonstrates respect for
                        colleagues and takes on
                        outside opinions

Commitment- She shows dedication to the
                        company and a passion to succeed

Integrity -   Dorcas is willing (there you go -
                        almost   a   literary   allusion

there....look it up !) to question
the status quo; gives
meaningful feedback

Suzannah then wrote a small piece at the bottom of the form and then asked me to read it and sign if I agreed or wanted to make my own comment - as if anyone actually reads this trite nonsense !

'Dora has been in the employ of the police for nearly a year and in that time, I have never had the need to chastise her or rebuke her in any way. Admittedly I have had very little interaction with her but what I have has been a pleasurable experience and I have always felt that I could trust her to mind her place and respect those above her, such as myself'
.........Suzannah Dowling

I couldn't resist, and so I wrote

'My name is Dorcas, Dorcas not Dora. I have been here for nearly a year and apart from having been duped into working here, having coffee thrown at me and then having to see Ms Dowling and a fat sweaty bloke going at it in her office, I haven't seen her. I get here on time, I do my work, and I go home. The pay is decent, and I can't say fairer than that....oh and my cat is called Tiddles......' Dorcas Goode

SD   Excellent Dora, that's that shit done for another year, you can go now

D   You owe me Suzannah. That's two chances you've had

And I got up and walked out of her office, noticing the large filing cabinet in the corner of the room where she put my appraisal form back with my Personnel file - interesting .

Terry's special guests (part one)

I was minding my own business, in the Custody Unit obviously, when Terry came over to me.

T.M   Morning Dorcas, how you doing pet?

D   Yep. Fine Terry, how are you?

T.M   I'm OK, but I'm about to get very busy. Apparently, there's some special guests arriving, and I get the impression that they won't be needing a bail sheet, if you know what I mean?

D   No. I'm sorry, I don't know what you mean

T.M   It means that these particular guests won't be going home tonight, well actually, if all goes to plan, they won't be going home for some considerable time

D   Oh right, and who are these special guests then Terry?

T.M   I can't really tell you Dorcas, you're 'only the cleaner,' but let's say you weren't. Let's say you were someone really important, someone really in the know. Who would you want it to be, who, given the choice, would you want in these cells, under my control? Go on Dorcas, we're coming towards the end now

D   The denouement if you will

T.M   Exactly, the denouement. We are coming to the end of our production , after all the excitement, the peaks, the twists, and turns, we ….

D   Are coming to the denouement, yes Terry, I get it, that's what a denouement means

T.M   Yes, I know that you know that, but does everyone know that?

D   I've no idea, possibly not, but anyway, back to your question. Who would
I wish to be in your cells, let's see.
Ted Heath

T.M   Agreed, but it's not him

D   Harold Wilson, James Callaghan, I don't know?

T.M   One day maybe, but not today. No. Think. Who has given you grief, who has made your life uncomfortable, miserable even, since you've been here - there's a clue

D   Is this in any particular order

T.M   Oh - stand by your beds - here comes the first

PC   Good morning, Sergeant. I am PC 6752 from another force.

T.M   Right. Understood. And how are you this fine morning PC 6752

PC   I'm alright as it goes really. Bit of a cushy number this morning. Got up a bit early, drove here, had a quick cup of tea, which was a bit rough to be honest

T.M   Often is. Should have called ahead, we could have got the proper stuff out. You know, as a thank you for all the mess you're clearing up today

PC   Ah, that's a shame. Anyway, lodge this little bloke here and off for brekkie - lovely. Can you recommend anywhere decent?

T.M   Oh yeah, there's lots of places around here. Well sort you out somewhere decent to go don't you worry. Now, to business. Do you want to bring him in? Just, by the way, before we get started, that's not going to go off, is it? That thing on your hip?

PC	No? What? This little thing - just for show really - I can show you a proper gun if you like later - they're all in the van
T.M	No. You're all right…shall we?
PC	Right you are. 6776
T.M	Eh?
PC	No, sorry, that's my mate - I was calling my mate. 6776?
PC2	Morning 6752, didn't I see you earlier?
PC	You did, you did, down the barrel, ey?
PC2	Yeh, down the barrel - better than up the barrel, eh?
T.M	Sorry to intrude, and I appreciate that's probably an inhouse joke or something, but could we put our dicks, sorry, guns away and wheel the accused over here please.
PC2	Sorry Sarge. Here you go.
T.M	So, good morning, and you are?
A	Oomph Omphaffer
T.M	Sorry, officer, I appreciate you're Firearms and all that, but is this all really necessary? I mean he's not the biggest bloke in the world is he. Trussed up like that? And the hood? Really?

PC2	Protocol, Sarge, protocol
T.M	Yes, I appreciate that, but now we're all here, inside here, and I presume he's been searched, properly searched, you know for little things that could be easily secreted anywhere
PC2	Oh yeah, like small bullets - stuff like that - hadn't thought of that - good one Sarge
T.M	I mean ….and wait for this….'he's always been a bit anal'
PC2	Ay?
T.M	You know, a bit anal? And now he needs to be properly searched…like properly searched - do you understand?
PC2	Oh yeah, and who's gonna do that then Sarge
T.M	I have just the person… PC Grimes?

A short time later a very cowed and slightly bewildered 'accused' came back to the Custody Desk, minus hood and handcuffs and walking very gingerly towards Terry, accompanied by the two firearms officers still laughing about how the accused probably had a 'bigger gun' at home than the one he brought here on this cold and frosty morning, and so on.

A   You've got a good one there Sergeant

T.M   What? PC Grimes, yeah, he's alright really John, he's a bit slow sometimes, but we're hopeful he may come around. You know he may even go on Firearms one day, who knows? Certainly, got the brains for it

A   Certainly enthusiastic about the old searching malarkey

T.M   Oh, yeah? Bit too enthusiastic, was he? He volunteered; you know?

A   Ah. That would explain things. I wouldn't mind, but aren't they supposed to wear gloves?

T.M   Gloves? Oh, yeah, that would probably be better, I'll speak to him and certainly, encourage him for next time

A   Next time?? Fucks sake Sarge, there's not going to be a next time is there. I'm not going through that again.

T.M   No. That's true. I bet you're hoping though, bearing in mind where you are likely to go, that PC Grimes doesn't suddenly transfer to the Prison

195

Service ey?

A   Too true. So, shall we?

T.M   Yep. OK. Can I have your name please?

A   John McAvitee

T.M   Thank you John. And do you know why you're here?

JA   Cos, I work here…ha ha !

T.M   Not for much longer I wouldn't have thought John. For fucks sake, whatever possessed you?

JA   Money.

T.M   Root cause of all evil John, money is

JA   One of the root causes Terry, it's just one of them, though the actual quote is 'for the love of money is the root of all evil'

PC2   Sergeant, sorry. This is John McAvitee, he's been arrested
today at his home address under the Prevention of Terrorism (Temporary Provisions) Act 1974

T.M   Really? Are you sure?
What section?

PC2   Erm….

T.M   Maybe not theft?

PC2   Erm… 6752???

T.M   Not maybe something in there about the Firearms Act of 1968 perhaps?

PC2   6752???

Terry took the second unnamed PC into his office and whilst there were no raised voices, I heard Terry whisper quite loudly

T.M   Listen, you jumped up, no dick, little air thief, if this goes south because you don't know the fucking law, I will take the weaponry in your van and shove each and every one of them up your arse so far you will need a darn sight more than a long arm to retrieve them. Go out and fucking do your job, do you understand?

PC2   Yes Sergeant

T.M   Yes Sergeant, no Sergeant... call yourself a fucking copper...all you want is to walk around with a gun on your hip and impress the ladies......have you seen any ladies here yet?

PC2   No Sergeant

T.M   No Sergeant. So, fuck off out of my office and do your job

The two officers came out of the office and after a little shuffling of his feet the unnamed PC said

PC2   Sergeant, this is John McAvitee. I have arrested him today at his home address on suspicion of theft and unauthorised selling of firearms

T.M Thank you officer. And did the accused make any reply after caution.

PC2 No Sergeant, not an actual reply as such, but there was a funny noise behind him and then...then this really strong smell of....

T.M Yes, thank you officer. It was probably the size of your weapon?

Mr McAvitee, you have heard what the officer has said. Is there anything you wish to say at this point.

JA No. Thank you Terry.

T.M Sergeant, Mr McAvitee, its Sergeant OK, sorry

JA No Sergeant. Thank you.

John McAvitee, presumably now the former Property Officer, was taken away and put in the female cell block, which I thought strange, until I noticed an armed guard at the gates and realised there were no women prisoners in the cells. I understood the whole female cell area would not need cleaning today as it was going to be quite busy.

Result ! One down. Time for a brew.

Listening at the door

The girl sat in the corridor outside the office of the Mother Superior. This was not a convent, but a Children's Home. A place for children who had no home and were now in the care of the nuns. They cared for the children but expected them to accept G…she couldn't bring herself to say it, or even think it. Accept that someone looked over them and guided them in their thoughts and deeds?

It was just nonsense. What the nuns described was surely just conscience - every person had one and every person would or should be led by it, plain and simple.

The girl held her breath and listened at the door.

Mother Superior	Young Siobhan Murphy, now there's a girl meant for the sisterhood
Sister Katherine	You are joking surely?
MS	No? Why? You don't think so? Why not? She's kind, polite, knows her prayers, knows her

	Bible inside and out - she'd be perfect, one day, obviously not yet she's only ten years old
SK	And that's the reason why. She is ten years old and yes, she knows her Bible inside out. But she's a nightmare in class, asks far too many questions, poor old Sister Theresa nearly had a stroke with some of them, and she's so argumentative, honestly, we need to keep an eye on her
MS	Questions? Questions are good, surely, an inquisitive mind is a healthy mind
SK	An inquisitive mind is a pain in the arse Mother Superior, forgive me, I will repent fully on Sunday, but the Lord himself would have told her to, what's the modern vernacular?
MS	'Desist my child?'
SK	No
MS	'Ask no more questions, be calm and be at peace my child?'
SK	Really? No, I think even the Lord himself would have told her to 'go f...'

MS	Sister Katherine, don't go there
SK	Well look, look at some of these questions - look here's one-'if Jesus is the Son of God, who is his Grandad?' And here - look - 'If Adam and Eve were the only people in the Garden of Eden, and they only had two sons....'
MS	Yes, I know that one, I do ask myself that one occasionally
SK	And what is the answer?
MS	That Adam and Eve were not real people but representations of man and woman as God created them
SK	So they weren't real then?
MS	Well yes, well no, but… this is not about me. Go on
SK	Siobhan asked Sister Theresa who wrote the Bible
MS	Oh dear Lord, here we go again. And what did Sister Theresa say, dare I ask
SK	Sister Theresa, who let's face it was born last century said, and I quote 'It is God's word, and no one else's. Do not doubt or challenge the word of God, for thou will be cast out of His kingdom and will burn in hell for all eternity'
MS	Sweet Jesus

SK	I know, it's not an answer that satisfied Siobhan, I mean it doesn't satisfy me, and I sort of know where Theresa was going with it.
MS	What did Siobhan say, dare I ask
SK	She said 'if it's God word why is it in English and not Hebrew'
MS	Fair enough question. Next
SK	'Was Jesus black?'
MS	Oh, and I'm going to have a free one here - 'oh fuck' - send her in

Sister Katherine wearily got up, stubbed out her Rothmans, brushed down her habit, well, brushed off her current habit's ash from her habit and stood. She was getting too old for this being a bride of God gig. It wasn't nonsense as such, just that the world was moving so quickly and children were so curious now they just didn't believe anymore, and it was so wearying. Oh, they believed in jazz and Glen Miller, but tell them that God was bigger and better than all of them and they'd laugh you out of town. It wasn't like the old days - the simpler days. Anyway, she'd done her bit, over to the Mother Superior now - let her have a crack.

'Siobhan Murphy. Front and centre'
'Yes Sister' said the ten-year-old girl and
stood up.
Siobhan knocked on the door, counted to ten and
then entered the Mother Superiors office. She
stood in front of the large walnut desk whilst the
nun sat in her enormous swivel chair with her
back to the girl. It was silent, so silent Siobhan
could hear the nun breath, she could hear a bell
toll somewhere in the village five miles away,
Christ it was so quiet in here that she could hear
the grass grow outside the window the nun was
looking through.

Siobhan thought that religion was not for her.
Even at ten years old she knew that it was all
made up. Faith, she reminded herself, and as
many others had said before, is belief
without proof.

Siobhan kept her dictionary with her at all times
as she loved words, and she always used them
wisely. She tried, every day, to learn a new
word, its meaning, and how to use it in her
general conversation. Unfortunately, today's
word had been faith and Sister Theresa was now
having a lie down in the nurse's room due to
Siobhan expressing her doubt in relation to this

word and its religious interpretation. Sister Katherine had just walked her straight to the Mother Superiors office - 'dodging a bullet' was what she had said she was doing. 'Lacking faith in her own ability to argue' is what Siobhan thought.

The Mother Superior swivelled lazily around and propped her feet up on her desk. It was an unusual pose for a nun, but she thought if this was going to be a long one, she needed to be comfortable. There was a bottle of scotch in her bottom drawer, but the child was only ten - let's see where this goes first before resorting to that, she thought, although she was tempted.

MS   So, Siobhan. What's up? What's the skinny?

SM   Good morning, Mother Superior, I trust you are in good health?

MS   Yes child, I am, thank you

SM   I will take your word for it, as I believe you and have complete trust and confidence in what you say as regards your health.

MS   As you should. Why wouldn't you? I am fine. A little stiffer in the mornings, and a little quicker to tire in the evenings, but ….hold on. I am asking the questions

SM   Certainly Mother Superior. Sorry.

MS   Now. I understand you have questions about our way of life, our choices and religion generally

SM   No. Not really.

MS   No? Oh well, off you go then. You'll stop asking questions then will you, you'll stop upsetting the other nuns, especially Sister Theresa - she's not well, you know, and you could tip her over the edge

SM   Then she'll be with her G won't she

MS   God?

SM   Yes, G. She'll be with Him, and she'll be happy won't she…I mean if you believe all of that.

MS   What do you mean, 'if you believe all that?' Are you saying you don't? Is that what all of this is about? You don't believe in God?

SM   Can I be honest?

MS   Of course my child, this is what will one
     day be called a 'safe space'

SM   Then no. I don't believe in G. I more
     subscribe to the Greek philosophy that
     there are many gods, each with their own
     specialism. And that you have to make
     your own way in the world and not anger
     the gods but appease them.

MS   What do you know of Greek
     philosophy Siobhan

SM   I've been reading Mother Superior. It
     really is quite illuminating.

MS   Talking of such things, you would have
     been burnt at the stake for heresy a few
     years hundred years ago. You can't go
     around saying things like that

SM   Why not? Are we not here to learn?

MS   Well yes. But within strict boundaries.
     We can't have you going around citing
     Greek philosophers like they were
     real people

SM   But they were real people - they more real
     than some bloke who walked on water,
     raised the dead and supposedly came back
     to life himself after being shut up in a
     cave for three days. It was only three days
     though - do you know about Socrates

MS   Yes of course I know about Socrates - old white bloke, talked a lot, a lot of them did you know?

SM   Socrates asked questions. Now I'm obviously not comparing myself to him, but he was sentenced to death for asking too many questions.

MS   No he wasn't. He was sentenced to death for corrupting the youth
of Athens

SM   Yes, for urging them to ask questions and not just accept what they were told. He didn't do anything wrong, apart from ask questions.

MS   But some questions should not be asked

SM   Like what?

MS   Like that one. Look, you are obviously an intelligent girl. So, study, learn well and, well…keep silent regarding the religion thing, and when you leave here
you can ask as many questions as you like. You really could be anything you want to be, you know that don't you?

SM   Socrates died by his own hand. He drank hemlock rather than remain silent. Do you know they would have freed him if he'd agreed to remain silent. I'm sorry I
just can't.

MS   I appreciate that you have not introduced
        new Gods into the building, but you have
        upset the minds of the younger children
        who accept that God exists and that there
        is only one true God.

SM   True, and Father Christmas, and the Tooth
        Fairy - Mother Superior, I'm really sorry, I
        don't mean to argue, I really don't, but
        faith is having complete trust and
        confidence in someone or something
        and…well, I just don't have that

MS   Understood, and that's perfectly fine.
        Until you do have complete trust and
        confidence in the Lord you will eat alone,
        study alone and sleep alone. Be gone and
        think on that. Your new room has already
        been prepared for you.

And with that Siobhan left the room and the
Mother Superior reached for the bottom drawer.

Siobhan had often thought of that conversation
with the Mother Superior, she thought it had gone
quite well, all things considered. But perhaps she
should have told her that there was nothing she
preferred more than her own company. She was
currently sharing a room with five other girls, two
of whom had come perilously close to being

strangled in their sleep, they just didn't know it yet. Perhaps Siobhan should tell them both that she was thinking of strangling one of them, but that hadn't decided which one yet. Just to see what would happen.

Siobhan went to her new room, closed the door, and sighed a happy, contented sigh. She pulled her suitcase from beneath the bed and sat cross legged on the floor with her old friend Socrates. Well, it wasn't actually a book by Socrates, as, as everyone knew he never wrote anything down. It was a book by his student Plato called the Apology of Socrates. Siobhan thought it good in places and was looking forward to reading the 'sequel' - a book called Crito, which dealt with the injustice of Socrates' imprisonment. When she'd read both again, she may very well have another chat with the Mother Superior.

Terry's special guests (part two)

I was cleaning on the ground floor one morning when all of a sudden there was a commotion coming from the busiest place in the station - my favourite place, and perhaps yours - the Custody Unit.

My mop found its way swiftly across the floor and stopped, all of its own just a short distance away from Terry's desk - honestly, does this man never take a day off, I thought.

D   Morning Terry, what's going on? What's all the hullabaloo?

T.M   Morning Dorcas, you don't want to be in here today, you really don't.

D   Why? What's happened?

T.M   Nothing yet, and as I understand it nothing did. Apparently, someone is coming in, and there will be a reception committee awaiting them, although as I understand it, I will be otherwise engaged with something really important and didn't see or hear anything.

D   Oh dear, though I don't fully understand, I think maybe I should be elsewhere as well, don't you. This doesn't sound like something a mere cleaner should be involved in, or even aware of

T.M   Oh, no, Dorcas, you see I will apparently be helping you with restocking your cleaning cupboard, just out of the Custody Unit, and therefore couldn't possibly know what did or didn't happen.

D   Ah, I see. Will this restocking take a long time Terry, I've got a million things to do today

T.M   No, it shouldn't really, though it depends how many others weren't in the Custody Unit at the time the accused landed

There was suddenly an urgent need for Terry and me to restock my cleaning cupboard and it later transpired that six, unoriginal colleagues of Terry also had the same idea and helped us, just like that.

I have mentioned before a thing which is locally called a crucifix run, and today I didn't see it in action, what with restocking my cupboard and not looking over the shoulders of all the others who were apparently there and helping me.

A man dressed in tight orange trousers and a frilly yellow shirt was carried bodily, in the aforementioned crucifix position and delicately deposited in a holding cell. This area was just outside the main cell block and away from other detained prisoners.

The delicately deposited man lay on the floor and said to the assembled six officers, who weren't obviously there - as it were....you get the gist?

'Hang on lads, let me just assume the position ' and curled himself into a foetal pose on the ground, hands over head, chin tucked in.

The six officers, chosen from an enormous selection pool of volunteers then proceeded to set about the man, head, body and legs. I know Baz Sturgess deserved a good kicking from time to time, and I would have liked to join in, but did he deserve this?

The room he was in was very small, hardly enough for the number of people it now contained, and there was now such a flurry of fists and boots it was hard to tell where one person ended, and another began.

Eventually the assault stopped and those involved casually walked away.

The two arresting officers stubbed out their cigarettes on the wall outside, entered the Custody Unit and picked DC Sturgess up off the floor and walked him over to Terry's desk. Fortunately, my cleaning cupboard was now fully restocked, and I thought other areas of the Unit needed my attention - such as the holding cell which had a decidedly sticky floor it seemed.

PC   Grimes Good morning, Sergeant, room for a little one?

T.M   Certainly, PC Grimes, and who do we have here then?

PCG   This fine specimen of humanity used to be Detective Constable Barry Sturgess

T.M   Now then PC Grimes, let's stay professional, shall we? Baz? Is that you? I hardly recognised you. Whatever happened to you? I've only just come into the room as you could probably see, out of your one good eye, but trust me, I will make sure no harm comes to you, and that no ill befalls you whilst you're in my custody, I hope you understand that. I appreciate your ears look a bit chewed up at the moment, but I'm told the ringing in them stops after a few hours.

Now, in all seriousness, as I put pen to paper, what on earth happened to you?

BS   I understand that I fell down the stairs, repeatedly

T.M   I'll just put the lid on my pen again and point out that we're on the ground floor.

BS   No, not fell, I tripped, I tripped over in the shower, of my house, long before I was politely awoken and arrested calmly by PC Grimes here

T.M   Oh dear Baz, that's a shame, dangerous things showers, and did you perhaps then fall down your own stairs as you rushed to answer the door in case it was someone important?

BS   Yes, that's right, now you mention it, you know how tricky stairs can be, first thing in the mornings, especially with wet feet.

T.M   I do. And is that what you want me to write down Mr......?

BS   Sturgess, Sergeant, yes, if you wouldn't mind. You know, in case anyone notices

T.M.   Yes, very well, here comes my pen lid off again. Right. PC Grimes. Why is this person before me, what is it that he is accused of? And keep it professional, it's not like we're being recorded, but keep it simple ey?

PCG	This....gentleman was arrested by me at his home address on suspicion of dealing drugs, specifically cocaine.
T.M	Oh, right? On how many occasions?
PCG	Oh, I only arrested him once Sarge
T.M	No, you thick f..., no officer I meant.... Oh, don't worry. No doubt the jungle drums will make it about a million times, by the end of the day. So, Mr Sturgess, you understand why you are here?
BS	Yes, Sergeant. I do
T.M	And is there anything you would like to say to the alleged offence, for which you have been arrested, and so far, properly treated?
BS	No thank you Sergeant. Bail?
T.M	Forget it.
BS	Segregation when I get to prison?
T.M	Not my decision Mr Sturgess, but if I had anything to do with it, not a chance
BS	Fair enough.
T.M	Oh PC Grimes, if you could just ask the cleaner to vacate the holding area, please, that particular Forth Bridge may need painting later, but at the moment I doubt it's worth cleaning just yet, as I hear another special guest coming my way. Cell one for Mr Sturgess please

The soon to be former Detective Constable was placed in the first cell on the left-hand side. The first cell on the right-hand side would shortly be occupied by someone he knew very well.

PC Willis	Sergeant, are you free to accept another person into custody?
T.M	Yes, but just a moment please. I think the cleaner's cupboard needs unstocking first - Dorcas have you a moment please.

At this, six different officers from before, who weren't there and didn't walk past Terry and I, didn't walk into the Custody Unit and didn't take their place near the back door.

The same unseen, unheard assault of a soon to be former colleague didn't take place and as Terry walked back into the Unit he pointed me towards the holding cell, and apologising, asked me to do as good as a job as I could and if I needed any more cleaning material to let him know as my cleaning cupboard was seemingly overstocked.

PCW   Good morning, Sergeant, this is Francis Fairbourn who…can you stop dripping all over the floor please, for goodness sake, some of it got on my boots

FF   ffnerph frphhfp

PCW   Yes, well, that's as may be, but I've only just polished them. Sorry Sergeant, this is Francis Fairbourn who was arrested by me on suspicion of supplying controlled drugs, namely cocaine, handling stolen goods and for the illegal selling of firearms. He made no reply to caution.

FF   Well, I tried to reply to caution.

PCW   Did you? I'm sorry, I didn't hear you. What was it you were trying to say, can you remember, or did you need another couple of minutes in the holding cell to refresh your memory

FF   No. Come to think of it, I don't think I made any reply. Sorry. My mistake

PCW   Oh, OK then. Which cell Sergeant

T.M   Cell two please, hang on a minute, where was Mr Fairbourn arrested, his home address I take it?

PCW   Well it was someone's home address, but it wasn't his. I believe the lady in question is in a car outside awaiting being booked into custody?

T.M   OK then. Cell two it is, and I wondered if you could slowly put him in the cell, ensuring you make as much noise as you can, just in case any other residents are trying to sleep.

PCW   Sarge?

T.M   You'll see

The next person coming into custody really did need a good kicking. If ever there was a person who needed to be brought swiftly down to size, it was this woman. She had not had much to do with me during my time here, if I'm honest, but she had made what interaction we had had much worse than it needed to be. I didn't like the woman and it was plain she did not like me. I hadn't done her any harm, all I had done was, be honest and direct with her. I spoke my mind to her, when asked, and sometimes not, but it was clear she felt she was better than me. She had no qualifications to speak of, was apparently absolutely useless at her job and had worked her way up the staff chain of command based on her looks and her sycophantic ways. But apart from that I had no issues with her and wished her all the best. I also wished at that moment that there had been more female volunteers in the selection pool.

I think she knew she was in trouble and that she was likely to go to prison as she constantly wept and wailed while Terry booked her in. There were no more airs and graces with FLAPS this morning and her days of being in charge of almost everything non-police at the station were long gone. I think that fact had dawned on her earlier that morning when her door had apparently come flying off its hinges at about six o'clock and a number of masked police officers ran up the stairs.

She would not do well where she was going and the sooner, she realised she was no better than anyone else the easier it would be for her. She had a lot to learn, and I would love to teach her someday. I had been 'inside' before and though it wasn't pleasant, it was survivable if you kept your head down, didn't upset anyone, and bided your time.

I'm nicked

Terry had retired from the police, and it had left me a little lost to be honest. Oh, I still went into the Custody Unit, but I had so enjoyed our almost daily chats over a cup of decent tea, and I missed them terribly. Why it was that tea formed such an important part of a policeman's day I would never know, but as I went about my work, my cleaning work, I saw hundreds of mugs, cups and other receptacles left lying about the station – poor old Ida ! It did make me wonder what chats had happened over those cups of tea, what decisions had been made, what plots had been hatched and who had gained and who had lost whilst those brews were being sipped.

I was just making my own brew in the front office when someone walked through the front door whom I had not seen before. They were obviously of rank as they had several people around them doing things for them, opening doors, carrying briefcases and so on and my immediate thought was that I was in trouble.

I knew that following the arrests of FLAPS and the others my time would come. Even the most basic of investigations into the sale of guns and drugs would lead back to the cash and counterfeit notes seized at the same time and it was only due to Larry's leaving the Drugs Squad that things had taken as long as they had to be found.

As I prepared to give myself up to what was most likely a hunting party for me, all I could think of was 'have I left the kettle on at home?', 'did I feed the cat'. I knew that the day would arrive when I would have to 'take a nicking' as the expression went. I had been arrested before, but that was sort of sudden and unexpected, as I had been in a bank trying to get a large sum of money out of someone else's account when I had been 'rumbled' by staff. The police were called, and I was arrested in the bank. I had been interviewed and bailed to Court. Subsequently I served a very long year for fraud, but this time it would be a lot longer, and I just hadn't really had time to prepare myself for that. I should have ran when I had the chance, I had taken the cash out of the station and that was being safely salted away for the good cause I had in mind for it. But I knew that if I had run, had tried to 'make a break for it' I would only be making things so much worse and that things may then be investigated by better detectives than they appeared to be here, people with more experience and know-how than the ones I'd seen at Sandford.

No. Better that I stand and face what was coming. I readied myself and listened in to the conversation going on at the front counter as one of the hunting party approached the Desk Sergeant, who was Bob Fitzwilliam, the first policeman I'd met when I started working here.

HP1   Morning. Let us in Sergeant.
BF   What? Just like that? I don't know who you are, mate? Do you want to at least show some ID?
HP1   Do you not recognise who we are? Don't you know who my boss is?
BF   God? He seems a fair bet, unless of course you're not of that persuasion.
HP1   What? What persuasion? What are you on about? Open the door right now
BF   I mean if you're religious or not. That persuasion. Look. Look at things from my perspective. Some smart suited arse rocks up at my station and demands to be let in, and when challenged says 'Do you not recognise who I am?', which is odd,

because if I did know who you were we wouldn't be having this conversation now would we? You would be through that door and away to do God knows what to God knows who?

HP1   So you know we are from PSD then?

BF   Is that what you're calling yourselves now then is it? PSD. Let me think, let me think about what that acronym means...Pencil Swirling Dicks? Police Suicide Department? I know, I know, I've got one....

HP1   Try this, Sergeant. You know we are from the Professional Standards Department, formerly the Complaints Department and you either open the door and let us in or we will be swirling your dick into a charge for insubordination?

BF   Listen mate, it's not the fucking army anymore. You're no longer a Sergeant Major in the Royal whatever's. You're just a Sergeant like me. And, if I do open the door without you all showing me some form of identification then no doubt, you'd charge me with that. So, ID ? Yes, or no?

At which point Superintendent Michael Swift placed his identification card on the desk before the Sergeant.

BF   Fair enough Sir, you can come in, but your trained monkeys will have to show some ID, we get all sorts just wandering in through here.

The Superintendent nodded and the others with him immediately produced their warrant cards and were admitted to the station

BF   Mind the steps boys, hate for you to trip over. I doubt anyone would help you.

Having escorted the four PSD officers through the front office the Desk Sergeant returned.

BF   I'd make myself scarce if I were you, Dorcas. I don't know what's gone on, but you know it won't be good news they're bringing.
D   That's OK Bob, there's no point running. Could I ask you to do me a favour, as I may be gone some time.
BF   Oh, right? Going on hols then, are we?

D   Yes. Sort of. Could you put my mop and
        bucket away for me please, I need to go
        and make myself presentable.

BF   Oh, you sly thing- you're going on a
        date then?

D   With destiny perhaps if that's not being
        too dramatic

BF   Not with you?

D   Could I ask you to track down Terry
        McDermott and give this to him
        please. It's a sort of crib sheet of a few
        things I need doing at home.

And as I handed Bob a letter I turned and walked
back to a place I knew very well – the
Custody Unit.

When I got there the PSD officers were standing
talking to Phil McAvitee, the recently employed
Property Officer.

HP1   Listen you little fuckwit, we know it was
        you and the quicker you admit it the
        better, do you hear me mate?

PM   I honestly don't know what you're talking
        about officer. Seriously.

HP1   I love it when people say 'honestly' and
             'seriously'. They never mean
             what they say, and when they do speak it's
             never serious or honest. Just cough it
             McAvitee and we can all go home

PM   I don't know what that means – cough it?
             Cough what? Is this one of
             those medical examinations? I'm not
             going to have a gloveless search like
             my cousin did, am I?

HP1   What the fuck are you talking about mate?
             I'm not going anywhere near
             your…your… look, we're here to
             interview you about the missing money.
             That's what I'm talking about. Christ
             knows what you're talking about or what
             you get up to in your spare time.

PM   Oh right. Well, why didn't you say? Now
             what is it you want me to cough.
             We threw it away.

HP1   Threw it away? You threw it away? You
             threw away five hundred
             thousand pounds worth of cash? Why on
             God's green earth would you do that?

PM   Well I didn't….but I sort of said that she
             should…it had been there ages, and I'd
             sent memos to everyone – you know
             'move it or lose it' type memos. I never

got a reply, so it was cluttering up the place. She...she

D   It's alright Phil. It's OK. Officer, you need to speak to me

PM   And why would I want to speak to the fucking cleaner, pray tell.

D   For someone who uses the Lord's name in vain as much as you do, you are not what I would describe as a Christian person, are you, young man?

PM   Just who do you think you're talking to love, you're just the cleaner, do you know who I am?

D   I would like to speak to your Superintendent, alone. It will be the easiest interview he's ever had I can assure you. But if I have to deal with you, Sergeant then you will get nothing, nada, rien, zero. Do you understand? Do you know what this will mean for you?

PM   Go on.

D   It means you will have to work for a living and actually investigate something for a change, rather than just browbeat poor unfortunates, like Phil here into admitting something, anything, just for your figures.

Now run along little boy, and get the proper
 policeman, there's a good chap
At this the Sergeant walked over to his
Superintendent and spoke briefly to him.
The beginning of my term of incarceration
walked slowly towards me with an unbelieving
look on his face

SS   Good afternoon, madam, I understand you
      would like to speak with me?
D   Yes, if you would step into my office
      alone, I will help you resolve this mess.

We sat down at chairs I had often sat in when I
was giving advice to others or trying to find the
one, I was looking for to help me - oh how I
missed Pete, how I missed his idle chatter and his
way with words. I did also briefly consider
getting 'my solicitor' into the forthcoming
interview, but that may put him in a difficult
position, and I thought the outcome would be the
same anyway. Best to just get on with things.

D   So Superintendent. A fact for a fact, yes?
SS   What? What on earth? Are you serious?

D   Look. A fact for a fact. Sort of an honesty test if you will. I will tell you all I know about what I know, and you will have a tick in the box. What do you say?

SS   I would say that if you have stolen five hundred thousand pounds from the police station you are in serious trouble madam. That is a fact.

D   Well, I agree, I would be. Does that mean that I would be in half as much trouble if I had only stolen two hundred and fifty thousand pounds from the station then?

SS   Well. No. You would still be in serious trouble. The same trouble,

D   Oh, so if I stole a million pounds ....

SS   Can we get to the facts please Mrs?

D   Ms

SS   Oh God ! A feminist

D   No. You're wrong there. I am not a f feminist. I am just an independent woman in charge of her own destiny. I am aware of the likely outcome of this interview, but I need to know exactly, and I mean exactly, what it is you are investigating. No mind games, no...'is there anything else', because the moment you ask me that, the interview will be over, do you understand?

SS   You really have got some....

D   Don't say balls, please don't say balls.
Use your vocabulary - use your
words - say audacity, nerve, boldness,
anything but balls.

SS   Nerve then

D   Yes, perhaps I have. Now. A fact for
a fact ?

SS   Alright I will play your game. We are
investigating the theft of five
hundred....sorry two hundred and fifty
thousand pounds from this police
station and know that Phil McAvitee and
his cousin are responsible for that
theft. Fact.

D   No it's not. Have you any proof that they
stole it? Have they admitted anything to
you? Bearing in mind John has gone away
for a long time, don't you think he'd clear
his plate whilst there?

SS   Well yes, I see what you're saying. No, he
hasn't made any admissions. Yet. I would
have thought though with a little time and
a bit of gentle persuasion perhaps the new
McAvitee would cough to it soon enough.

D   Superintendent. One day this style of
policing will be looked back upon, and
they will tell tales of people like you.

Flash suits, shiny shoes, but absolutely nothing between the ears. A fast car and a hard fist? Really? Is that what we want our police to be. Is that what we want the custodians of the law to be remembered for. There will come a day when having a chat with a policeman will be just that, and it will be conducted in open air, not down an alleyway whilst being held by the scruff of the neck and dangling two feet off the ground.

SS   That's as may be, but hopefully by that time I will be long gone and sunning myself in Torremolinos or somewhere just as exotic.

D   Really? A Superintendent's pension and the best you could come up with is Torremolinos. You really have no vision, do you?

SS   What's wrong with Torremolinos, all my friends go there, great golf there you know?

D   So having worked, and I use the term loosely, for many years and retired on a Superintendent's pension you basically want to play golf in Spain?

SS   Can't wait

D   Where have all the visionaries gone; I ask. Would you not agree that you have me here, waiting to admit what I have done?

SS   Erm. Yes. Hopefully

D   And as a small Chinese chap I know once said that 'if you chase two rabbits then you catch none'

SS   What are you on about?

D   What I'm saying is. Leave Phil alone. He has nothing to do with anything. Let him keep his job, he's actually quite good at it. If you agree to that then I will tell you everything I know about the cash that went missing from the station. Do you agree

SS   Go on then. Let's say I agree

D   Do you?

SS   Yes. OK. I agree. Tell me what you know

D   I took it

SS   And?

D   No. That's it. I took it. I took two bags out of the police station as they had been in the property store for ages, and no one was doing anything with them. Phil told me they were bags of counterfeit notes, and to throw them, but I knew one of them wasn't. I put them in the skips outside.

232

What happened after that I do not know

SS   Fact?

D   That's better than you knew before we met. So as per our agreement you can get one of your trained monkeys to interview me, properly and then ship me off somewhere out of the way. Agreed?

SS   And what if I say no Ms. What if I say that you fully and frankly admitted everything to me and just declined to sign my pocketbook.

At that I got up and stuck my head out of the door.

D   Officers? Could I borrow you a minute please?

PC Grimes   Certainly Dorcas

PC Harris   Coming Dorcas

PC Stevens-Davis   Hello Dorcas

The three officers stood inside the interview room, formerly my office and I asked them

D   Officers. Could you tell us what you just heard please.

PC Grimes opened his pocketbook and read verbatim

"Superintendent Swift then stated that he had been at the golf club with Superintendent Colin Bradshaw, snorting cocaine, and that whilst in the ladies' toilets he had heard police cars arriving. He then stated that he had climbed out of the toilet window and ran into the nearby woods, just past the 14th green."

PC Harris opened his and read

"Superintendent Swift then stated that he had often been at the golf club with friends and had regularly been supplied cocaine by the former DC Baz Sturgess for him and his friend Superintendent Bradshaw to consume in the toilets prior to playing golf"

PC Stevens-Davis then opened his book

"Superintendent Swift…."

SS   I get the gist Ms. Goode. Agreed. Agreed.

D   Thank you officers. I will contact you if I need you

I was then asked to wait whilst the trained monkey came into the room. I then made the same admission to the PSD as I had previously. I was then charged with theft and told, as I had expected that I would not be bailed.

Banged up

I had been on remand for about three months and had a cell all to myself. I didn't mind being in prison again. I was guilty as charged and once convicted I would probably get about five years inside, so any time I did on remand would automatically come off my sentence.

I had made myself quite comfortable, it was peaceful and quiet for the main part, No one bothered me, and I didn't bother anyone. I did my work, cleaning funnily enough, and when I came back at the end of each day, I had my books. They were arranged on my windowsill, in order of importance to me - books on Socrates, books by Plato, then Aristotle and so on. I was as happy as I could be and bided my time until my trial. It would be a guilty plea and then straight back to the Greek philosophers for me. Sometimes when people had long trials, they had their cells reallocated to remand prisoners and I couldn't have that - goodness knows who I would end up with. I could end up having to share with some common criminal !

My days of running around committing fraud had to end, I wasn't getting any younger and I couldn't keep changing names and changing towns. I did want to settle down, oh not with a man, no not that sort of settle down - I mean who would have me and then I had a brain wave I think it's called now. No, I wanted to settle down, in myself, to find a place that I could call home. I had not known a proper sanctuary since the children's home, and that had given me an idea.

Now I'm here and not going anywhere for the foreseeable future. I may as well tell you what happened.

I had been arrested for stealing the cash and counterfeit notes from the Property Store but as the police could not find the cash that was all I had been charged with.

As you know I had been moving the counterfeit notes into the bag marked 'cash' and vice versa. It had taken me some time but when I'd done it, I had had the problem of how to get the cash out of the police station.

I'd just about finished swapping it all over when people started getting arrested for supplying drugs and so that meant that the focus would more than likely return to the cash and counterfeit notes and so I had had to move quickly.

As things turned out I had the fates on my side one day - you see the Greeks did know a thing or two. When John had been arrested for selling guns the station had been left without a full time Property Officer and I had the fortune one day of bumping into the new person - Phil, who, it turned out was John's younger cousin. Yes, I know, I also wondered if he had the same surname as his elder. To be honest Phil was a little slow and just liked simplicity and order, apparently, he'd previously worked in a warehouse and liked everything just so. I had offered to help Phil tidy up a bit and he eagerly agreed for me to help him. We tidied, we swept and polished until the Property Store was almost gleaming. I asked Phil what he wanted to do with the bits and pieces in the 'caged bit' at the back. He said he didn't want to be anywhere near guns and asked me to give it a once over and to lob anything that looked like it didn't belong there and sort things out as I saw fit.

As I was sweeping and dusting in the cage Phil came in and asked if I'd like a cup of tea, and while he nipped off to the canteen I was on my own, legitimately in the cage, with my money and my useless bits of counterfeit paper.

'Today is the day' I thought and swung the bag containing the cash but labelled 'uncounted counterfeit notes' up and on to my shoulder. I then carried it out to the rear yard and dropped it into a skip. Having covered it with a load of boxes and paper I returned to the office and had a nice cup of tea with Phil.

Whilst we were chatting, I asked Phil what I should do with the enormous bag of cash we had our feet resting on.

Phil laughed and said 'oh, apparently that's been here for years. It's not cash, even though someone's written 'cash' on it, it's funny money

D   Funny money, what do you mean Phil?

P   Funny money, you know counterfeit currency. I've been trained to spot it; you open the bag and have a look.

I did as Phil had asked and pulled out what looked very much like a twenty-pound note from the bulging bag.

D   It looks genuine to me, shouldn't we put it all in the safe or something. I mean it's obviously real, look, it's got the Queens head on it, and she's not smiling - just like on the proper ones

P   Dorcas. I appreciate you're just the cleaner, and I don't mean to sound rude, I know I've only just started here, but you would be really easy to have over. Look, it's fake, I can tell. Bin the lot of it, bag, and all, I'm fed up with tripping over it.

D   Seriously? I mean shouldn't we ask someone. It might be…what's that word?

P   Evidence? No. It's been here for years. No one's coming back for that.

I hadn't the heart to tell Phil that it hadn't been there for years, but having sipped a bit of my tea, I did what any lowly cleaner would do. I did what I was told and dropped bag number two into skip number two and came back to finish my drink.

For the rest of the afternoon, I was on tenterhooks. I couldn't clean properly - not that I was very good at it to begin with; I couldn't talk properly, and each time I thought of all that money just sitting waiting for me, my legs would go weak, and I would end up clinging to the nearest desk, wall, or surprised police officer. Eventually I was sent home as I was 'obviously poorly', 'probably women's troubles' I heard someone say and to which I nodded weakly and left the building.

As it turned out that night was Terry's 'leaving do' and I had been invited. I couldn't miss seeing my old friend one last time and so I said I would be there but wouldn't stay long as I would have to be in early to clear up everyone's mess the next morning, which got a bit of a laugh from him.

Pete had given me a lift down in his works van and I had asked him to pick me up at about eleven that night after I'd had a drink and a dance with Terry.

The evening had gone smoothly, and I had had a chance to speak to Terry, putting a proposition to him. He'd previously said to me that he had no idea what he wanted to do when he retired but I said I had a few business ideas which might interest him. Terry had said he was not looking for much as his pension was good and just some small menial job would do. I said I would come back to him, wished him all the best until maybe I saw him again and left the building for the second time that day.

Having loaded the bags into Pete's van we left the yard with almost five hundred thousand pounds of cash and counterfeit notes in the back. We drove to the garden centre Pete now owned and stored the bags in one of his greenhouses until we had had a think about things.

When I had first met Pete, he had been an alcoholic and had wandered about the town bothering people. I had managed to sober him up, but he had kept his 'I am thy Lord' persona in his back pocket so to speak, and it had come in handy for following people around the town.

People went about their business and ignored the 'town drunk', the 'mad God bloke' and just carried on as if he wasn't there. I had asked Pete to follow certain people around the town and report back to me as to what they did. I then fed this information back to Terry who had alerted the proper people, proper Drugs Squad officers, to take over.

A Drugs Squad from out of town apparently couldn't believe their luck, they had the opportunity to take out another Drugs Squad, a DS and a DC who had been selling the seized drugs for their own profit.
I understand they couldn't believe their good fortune when they saw not only DS Frank Fairbourn and Barry Sturgess selling openly in the street but also to many rich and supposedly important people at the golf club.

As a result, twenty people were arrested for buying drugs from the police officers, but the best bit was catching the Chief Superintendent, old Lard Arse himself in the toilets sniffing cocaine off the cistern in the ladies loo. Why the ladies loo I've no idea, and it was never explained.

DS Fairbourn and DC Sturgess received prison sentences of ten years each whilst Colin Bradshaw escaped jail time but was sacked and had his pension taken from him. I wonder what he's doing now. I bet he's not playing golf at the club anymore, that's for sure.

I've saved the best one till last though, almost my sweetest moment during my short police career. Old FLAPS herself, old Suzannah with a z and an h was also arrested.

It transpired that whilst not the actual brains behind the operation, she was certainly heavily involved with everything that had gone on. The original drugs raid by an outside force had been scheduled for a particular day and when a call had gone into 'the boss' they found that he had taken the day off. Apparently, the Drugs Squad officers had then asked, 'who was the boss?' if the Chief Superintendent was away and had been put through to Ms Dowling. Not announcing herself with her position or grade she listened and took notes of when and where the raid was to take place. She had politely thanked the caller and then made a number of calls to ensure that whilst the drugs and cash etc would be found no person would be there to be arrested.

It also transpired that FLAPS had been dating DS Fairbourn for some time and that they had made a living off similar fortunate circumstances as and when they arose but this one was the big one, the one that could not be ignored. They had hatched a plan that when the drugs were seized, they would be stored at their station and as was the case someone within that particular Drugs Squad would carry out the investigation.

Poor Larry Stevens Davis was swiftly brought on to the Squad and assigned the case to deal with, with their full knowledge that it was way beyond his capabilities. They already had outlets for the drugs but were a little stuck as to what to do with the cash and counterfeit notes and felt it would be too suspicious if all the seized goods went missing too soon, and so they left those in the back of a Property Store for future use.

FLAPS was also involved in the sale of guns from the station as well. John had removed them, but it was FLAPS and Frank Fairbourn who sold them to various drug dealers inside and outside the town, putting them back in the hands of the very people they had been seized from in the first place whilst making a tidy profit for themselves.

I thought this would explain her opulent office, but it turned out that that was just straight over excitedness of being put in charge of a police budget, which I'm told often happens with people in high places.

As a remand prisoner I was allowed a phone call every day and my first had been to Pete Masterson. He was now doing well for himself and was running a small garden centre just outside town. He had started small, initially with a market stall selling all sorts of things, from pot plants to compost, from dibbers to garden spades. He'd done well to start things up from nothing and I had often wondered where he got his original stock from, but he seemed happy and we both watched his business grow until one day with a loan from a friendly Bank Business Manager, who just happened to be called Trevor, Pete had bought a run-down garden centre.

As I understand it Trevor was more than generous with the terms of the loan, some seven and a half thousand pounds, in that due to his now being in charge of the NPA's Pete wouldn't have to repay it for some years, if at all.

Pete and I had a good chat and after ensuring that everything was proceeding as planned. I wished him a good day and returned to my cell , after all Plato awaited me, and I couldn't keep the gentleman waiting now, could I ?

Had they known what I had done with the money I'd stolen and stashed at Pete's greenhouse, and what else I was up to whilst 'just a mere cleaner' it would have probably got me another five years in prison.

Well, I may as well tell you my other two schemes, I'm not up to much really, just sitting in my cell, waiting, reading, contemplating life generally and I know you won't tell anyone.

While I had been in FLAPS's office one day early on, I had seen a large filing cabinet in one corner and whilst busily cleaning it I had found that one of the drawers suddenly became open. I obviously had to make sure that the hinges were cleaned properly and in opening it further it revealed its treasures. The cabinet contained everyone's Personnel Files, as I suspected it might,

This particular drawer was devoted to senior staff and whilst I wasn't overly interested in their contents it did make amusing reading - the pompous words they all used whilst slapping each other on the backs or the bitter ones said about the same people whilst removing knives from their own.

Anyway, having cleaned that drawer I turned my attention to the others and found, in the bottom drawer, obviously, my own Personnel File, but strangely also four other blank files for my staff. So, I was supposed to have a 'small, tight knit group' under my supervision after all.

Looking at the dummy files I saw that they all looked like mine, all that was missing were my team's names, addresses, dates of birth, and, most importantly, their bank account details.

And so, I duly obliged and completed the necessary details, I took the details, did my best Suzannah Dowling signatures and dropped the 'Personnel File' update forms into her out tray.

If you remember Pete had been opening bank accounts around the town, obviously in false names and these accounts now contained the fruits of my invisible staff's hard work. And goodness did my staff do a lot of overtime. I knew this was a risky scheme and was likely to be discovered at some stage, but I had survived one station audit already and had 'cleaned' the money by asking Trevor to move it offshore, for later use. Even if the fraud was discovered the money would never be found and I was prepared to 'do the time' if ever arrested for it. I secretly hoped that it was discovered because I didn't know any officer at that station who could have untangled the mess I had caused and that made me smile.

I had let Pete know my ingenious plan early on, and whilst I didn't want to boast, I was quite proud of myself. It would all be for a good cause in the end, and I was happy that I would be helping other people for years to come, no one had been hurt and criminal money had been put to good use. Yes, a few laws had been broken but that was better than the uses police forces currently put seized cash to - I wondered how many Suzannah Dowling's there were up and down the country and how many reclining settees an office really needed.

As it turned out my scheme so impressed Pete that we agreed he should use it for all his new 'casual workers' at the garden centre. These casual workers were 'paid' in cash and were all accounted for in his books. Provided no one from the Tax Office actually visited the garden centre we would be in the clear. Pete then used the 'washed' cash to pay, in dribs and drabs, into accounts all over town, whilst remembering to mix the counterfeit notes into the deposits. If he was ever challenged, he knew he could explain his bad luck of being 'done' with the occasional dud note.

My second call was to Terry. He had retired a few months ago and had given me his number in case I ever needed anything. Terry had gone on holiday the day after he retired, as he said he would.

'One day working, the next one on a beach with a cold beer' and he had been true to his word. He'd even sent me a postcard from some foreign shore, and I was very jealous of him when I'd received it. I only had the imaginary shores of some Greek island to compare to Terry's actual one - Porta del Lobos de Mariana or something equally tropical.

I was contemplating my situation when I heard the jangling of keys outside my cell door.

Not exactly a play date

The sound of keys jangling outside your cell is never a good thing, unless it's to wake you up in the morning or just before visiting time.

In the case of one it's the start of a brand-new day, albeit that day started, every day at six o'clock and for me meant a mop and bucket being launched into my ensuite by some half-asleep guard with today's instructions of where to start cleaning.

It was either

'Floor D, puke near D24' - lovely

Or

'Floor C, shit inside C31' - what a wonderful way to start one's day, but that was the life of a cleaner. Why, oh why couldn't I have said I was a cook when I was admitted to this place. Then it would have been

'Good morning, Chef. We wondered if you could whip us eggs benedict this morning, you know, just for three hundred girls'

Or

'Good morning, Chef. Lovely spread last night we particularly enjoyed the lamb tagine, where was that from again'

But no. This morning I had already been out and cleaned up whatever expulsion people didn't want in their cells, their corridors, or in the case of some of the guards - in their offices. The staff really should know better, sometimes with them I just felt like I wanted to mop up their detritus and shove it back in their offices, make them work in it for a day, see how that grabbed them. It's strange the word offices and orifices are very similar....now can I amend my last statement?

The last time keys jangled near me on a Friday it had been for my neighbour Jocelyn. I had no idea what she was in for, but her visitor had been a solicitor who had served her some paperwork. Afterwards she came to see me as she was a bit upset.

J   Cath, can I talk to you? I've had these shoved in my face and I don't know what to do

CT   Duck?

J   What?

CT   Duck, Jocelyn. I always duck if someone tries to launch something at me

J   Yeah, but they weren't launched, were they? They were shoved. From right up close, I couldn't avoid them

CT   Let's have a look. See what all this confusion is about shall we. What are they Jocelyn

J   That's the thing, I don't know. I can't read

CT   You can't read? What do you mean you can't read

J   I can't read alright. It's like at the moment you can't hear, I don't make a big deal out of it, I just accept it. Can you read them for me please?

And so, I sat and read through the papers. It made for very sad reading. It was almost like a dear John Letter if you were away on the Front, in the trenches of some muddy French village during a World War One battle. If you received that then you knew you had nothing to lose. And it's strange because I got the feeling that Jocelyn had

known what this paperwork was and probably
thought similarly.

CT	Jocelyn. You said you can't read at all
J	That's right
CT	Is that true
J	Not exactly, why?
CT	Well I notice what I think may be a couple of drops of blood on page six
J	He deserved it
CT	Who did?
J	The bloke what brung them here
CT	Brought. The bloke who brought them here. Who was he
J	Little bloke, shitty suit, all sort of shiny and last year. Slaphead, no balls. Just shoved them at me and tried to run out of the room.
CT	But you caught him. I take it he was a solicitor
J	No, solicitors' clerk, yeah, not even a proper solicitor, fucking bloke
CT	These are divorce papers, as I think you well know. Jocelyn, can I just ask what is it you are in for
J	One count of GBH on my husband
CT	Is that all?

J   Well probably two counts of GBH now. Oh, and Miss Westman says could you do a bit of a clean-up in the visitor's room please, it's a bit messy what with all that bloke's blood, and possibly a few teeth?

I had been thinking back to that time and wondering what could cause the jangling of the keys mid-morning, and on a Friday as well. Court day....oh no, no please....it couldn't be a roommate.

I knew the place was filling up - it was only a small remand centre for women - a fairly new concept - (a) that women committed crimes that were worth locking them up for pending trial and (b) they really shouldn't be mixed in with the men. If ever there was a way to overpopulate an establishment, then that was it. Thank G they changed that, but this was my cell, I shouldn't have to share it with anyone.

The jangling stopped and the door opened with the obligatory 'Taylor. Back to the wall' barked into my sanctuary. I really did feel like that about my little 12'x10' space, my little 12'x10' piece of heaven. It was mine and I had made it just the way I wanted it. On one wall I had pictures of places I had been and where I wanted to go - my travel wall as I called it. The pictures were mainly of Greece, but there were other places as well.

The guard entered with a sneer on her face

G   So, Taylor. Are you ready for a play date?

CT   No Miss, not really

G   Tough. You've got one, at least until you get sentenced and shipped off to somewhere else

CT   Miss. This is not right. I specifically asked for a single, not a twin .
        Surely there has been some mistake? Maybe a double booking? Could we check the register?

G   Shut up Taylor and scoot your things over, or I'll do it for you. Woodman?

CT   Sorry?

G   Shut up Taylor, not you. Woodman?

W   Yes Miss? Here

G   Yes, I know where you are since I told you to stand there. Now. get in here

The woman outside the cell, my cell was stooped over and wore the customary 'hoodie' sweatshirt a lot of the women now favoured. Consequently, I couldn't see her face, but by her walk, a shuffling scuffing type of forward movement, I envisioned her to be about seventy years old.

As the woman approached me, she flung her hood back and both she and the guard cheerfully shouted

'Surprise !'

CW   Hello, I'm Carole Woodman - your
       new roomie !
CT   FLAPS ! No, no, Miss, this cannot be
       right, please, anyone but her. I'll take that
       psycho that's just landed, you know the
       one who chopped up her boss and tried to
       eat him, her, I'll take her. Please Miss
       don't make me share a room with FLAPS
G   Why do you call her FLAPS?
CT   It used to mean something - in a
       former life
G   Oh, right? And what did FLAPS mean?
CT   It doesn't matter Miss. It's a long time ago.
       Welcome 'Carole', I'll just rearrange
       the cell

CW   Thank you Dorc….Cathy? Cath?
           Or Catherine?
CT   Cath is fine.

The guard left us and slammed the door, chuckling as she did and muttering to herself - 'FLAPS. I know what that means now - Fucking Listen and Possibly Survive. She ain't gonna make it'

FLAPS in trouble

FLAPS had been sent to the remand centre, like everyone else, pending her trial. When charged, she had said that she would 'fight it all the way', which were brave words at the time, and I think said more for effect than any intent. She had been in charge of the police station and had abused her position to the fullest extent. She was in trouble, and she knew it.

When the door to what was now our cell slammed shut, she flung herself at me and wept. Good grief I thought, women as well - what am I, a mother hen? Why does everyone automatically think I will solve their problems? Have I just got that sort of face?

CT   Calm down, calm down…FL…err Carole
CW   I'm sorry Dorcas, sorry Cath, I'm sorry, I'm sorry for the way I treated you, for the way I was, I didn't mean any harm by it, honestly.

CT Well. That's for later Carole. For the time being we need to toughen you up a bit. You won't survive in here if you go weeping and wailing on your first day now, will you?

CW How do you survive? How do you know how to survive? And why are you Cath Taylor? I thought you were Dorcas Goode.

CT And I thought you were Suzannah Dowling, with a z and an h? What was all that about?

CW I just thought it sounded better than my real name. I was born Carole Woodman but changed it, well sort of legally when I went for top jobs, you know it just sort of sounded better. What about you?

CT I was born Cath Taylor (I lied) but as I needed jobs I had to get away from that name. It had....history, you might say. A previous history. I wouldn't have been able to get a job in the police station with previous convictions now, would I?

CW Oh, you'd be surprised. I was in charge of Personnel Files and there were some right wronguns working there I can tell you.

CT	Yes. I know. It's just a shame that they weren't rooted out before they did what they did. It would have saved a lot of problems.
CW	I know, and some of that may be my fault Cath.
CT	Really? Just some of that?
CW	Look. I don't want to dwell on the past. We need to work together if we are going to get through all this.
CT	That is a massive presumption on your part Carole, why would I want to 'work with you'. All you've ever done to me is treat me like a second-class citizen, like I was nothing, so why would I help you. What could you possibly do for me?
CW	I'd pay you?
CT	Now you're talking.

Carole and I agreed that I would help her, at least until one of us left, either after our trials, or in the event of one of us moving cells. It was often the case that for seemingly no reason, people were moved from cell to cell. I think the guards liked seeing us unsettled, but sometimes it had the effect of unsettling the whole floor, so it happened less now.

I said that I would help Carole and in return she would help me with business, or more to the point, of how to run a business. I had big plans for the future, and I needed to know how a business ran from the bottom upwards. There would come a day when I would need some expertise to keep one step ahead and apparently for many years Carole Woodman in her guise as Suzannah Dowling had fooled everyone and done just that. She had juggled budgets and kept auditors happy, and it was only due to greed that she had been discovered.

It transpired that in addition to being involved in the selling of guns and drugs she had been involved in, she also had been stealing from the police budgets. She had done this, she said, for many years and as a consequence had had an opulent lifestyle all bought and paid for by the local Police Authority. She was almost proud of her success, and I had to remind her that in here, outward pride was not a thing to flaunt. She would be better off not saying what she had been charged with or making something up that more fitted her - like mass shoplifting or tax evasion. I also had to remind her that she was in here with everyone else, so she wasn't that successful, was she?

We had our evening meal in the cell as Carole said she couldn't face going out and mixing with a load of criminals in the canteen. Again, I reminded her that she was also a criminal and to stop acting like Suzannah Dowling, as that would only lead to trouble. I still didn't like Carole, I didn't trust her, but felt that we had to get along to a certain extent as I was bunking with her so I couldn't really get away from her. I think the guards knew our previous roles and either for a joke or as a bet they had put us together. Either way, I wasn't happy with the arrangement, but thought I should make the most of it. Carole also was paying her way with her business advice, so it sort of made sense, at least for a while.

The morning after Carole had arrived would be a busy day for her. She would have to be allocated a job, enrol for any courses or activities she wanted and make any phone calls to loved ones or solicitors. It was always important to let as many people know where you were as prisoners often got 'lost' in the system and this was very distressing for relatives and so on.

Carole slept the sleep of the dead, and I had to shake her roughly as the keys jangled once more outside our cell and the shout of 'Taylor, Woodman, up against the wall' rang out.

We stood against the back wall as a number of guards entered our cell but were then ushered outside. I had expected something similar to this, but on the first full day for Carole it was a bit extreme. Our cell was literally tossed from top to bottom, and it looked like a typhoon had run through it by the time the guards had finished. We were to remain outside the cell while this process took place and we stood one either side of the doorway, not saying a word.

Carole went to protest about it to one of the guards, but I managed to stop her, this would have been a foolhardy thing to do at all, let alone on her first full day here. She would have been charged with something, and if charged would have been immediately moved to solitary. She would not survive solitary.

After the guards left, we tidied up as best we could, and I calmed Carole down explaining to her that this is what they did. It was a test - to see if you would react and then give them reason to ....react back. Though the guards were all women it was a close call with some of them. I understand the Home Office now recruited directly from the Russian Women's shot putter team, and I'd always had my doubts about them, I was sure half of them were men.

The weeks passed and each week our cell was 'randomly selected' for inspection. I could see that Carole was getting angrier and angrier about it and would eventually fall for the guard's bait. She had had a couple of run-ins with other prisoners recently, one in the library of all places and had come off second best. I could see the change in her and though she said she had it under control I feared the worst. It was all I could do, when the keys jangled unexpectedly outside our door, to physically restrain her from going at the guards.

My worst fears were realised one afternoon when a number of guards entered our cell for a random search. Carole stood in the centre of the cell and refused to step outside as instructed and was unceremoniously moved by 'Olga' and three shot putting friends.

I pleaded with her to stay with me and just let them get on with it. We both knew they would not find anything as we had nothing in the cell of value or which could be counted as contraband, meaning prohibited. We were allowed a few bits and pieces but there were many things that were not.

I was happy nothing would be found and so stood against the wall outside my cell while four guards upturned beds, threw precious belongings about the room, and generally made mischief, as that's all I thought it was.

G1   Taylor? What's this?
CT   I don't know Miss, I'm not in there, I'm out here
G1   Taylor. Get in here
CT   Yes Miss

And I entered the room. One of the guards held in their hand something precious to me, something worth more to me than gold- it was my copy of The Republic by Plato, given to me by
Sister Bernadette

CT   That's my book Miss. Please be careful with it. It's very valuable

G2   Throw it here Suze, let me look at it

And the guards began to throw 'my precious' around the room, one to another and back again. I just knew that one of them would drop it on purpose and it would then be kicked around and get ruined, destroyed. I could not have that.

I was contemplating how best to keep the guards from baiting me when out of nowhere Carole came flying into the cell. She literally launched herself bodily into two of the guards, headbutting one of them full in the face, and as she was taken roughly to the floor by the other three, she kicked and bit as many limbs and shoulders as she could reach.

I could do nothing. My trial was due very soon and I could not risk getting involved. I would be charged with something, assault, or worse and I would never get out of prison if that happened.

I hated myself for it as Carole, FLAPS, had only been trying to help me, but I could not help her now. I didn't like the woman, had hated her, but at that moment I hated myself more. All I could do was tell her over and over to stop resisting, stop fighting, she could not win.

Eventually the struggle stopped, and Carole lay beneath three huge female guards. She had been punched, kicked, and hit with truncheons all over her body and she lay there panting as they, one by one got up off her. Carole's face was a mess and one of her eyes had already started to close. There was blood all over the floor. As she looked up at me, she smiled and said

CW   Know any good cleaners, Dorcas?

I nearly wept as I went to her aid, lifting her to her feet, but as I did, I was punched fully in the kidneys, and I dropped to the floor next to Carole. I whispered to her to just 'go with it and don't do anything stupid'.

She was going into solitary, and I feared how she would cope with being on her own for a minimum of a week.

Six days later my worst fears came to pass as the keys jangled outside the cell and 'Taylor, against the wall' rang out in the corridor.

Silently, three guards entered the cell and removed all of Carole's possessions, such as they were. The last thing they took was a polaroid of her on some sun-drenched island, smiling ,looking tanned and leggy with her arms around a larger gentleman, who perhaps didn't cope well with the sun as sweat glistened out of every pore. So, they had been in love after all.

Carole Woodman aka Suzannah Dowling had hung herself the previous night and had been found in the morning as cold as last night's untouched food that sat on her bunk. A suicide note addressed to me was found and eventually I was allowed to read it.

It read:-

Dear Dorcas, or Cath if you prefer,

I don't know what your name is, and it doesn't really matter what you call yourself, it's who you are that counts.

I was never good to you and for that I am truly sorry.

In these past few weeks, you have shown me what to do to survive, and somehow shown me, if not friendship, then comradeship, and for that I am so grateful. But I know that without you, when you get released, I will not survive on my own and I have made a choice to remove myself from that future suffering.

I know that I am in serious trouble and facing a number of my best years locked up for what I did. I have had a good life; I've enjoyed myself and I have been lucky to have had someone like Frank to share that life with. Please try and find him and tell him that I will always love him and for him to be strong.

Please also tell him to let you know where we first met and then I would like you to visit that place someday and raise a glass to me - I wasn't all bad, I promise.

Your friend, hopefully

Carole
X

The luck of the Irish

I had now been on remand for several months and after Carole's death I sort of went into myself. I had a single cell again, but that was small comfort knowing I should have helped her more. I should have stepped in and helped her when she was being assaulted by the guards. I had protested to the Governor about what had happened, whilst Carole was in solitary and begged him to release her as I feared she would do herself harm. I had meant cutting herself or something of that nature, but little did I know that Carole had planned so much worse.

The Governor told me that a full investigation would take place and that if any of the guards were in fact found to have been there as the inmate apparently ran repeatedly against the wall then they would be severely reprimanded. And that was it.

The following day I was advised in writing that the investigation was complete and that no action would be taken against any guard as there was no evidence of any assault having taken place. Indeed, two of the guards were to be commended for their swift action to prevent the inmate from doing herself or others, further harm.

I had to get out of this place. They had knowingly let Carole die. They knew she was not fit to be in here, let alone in solitary, but had done nothing to prevent her death. Admittedly, they were not responsible for her hanging herself, but they were responsible for putting her there in the first place, in a position to do herself harm. I found out that none of the hourly checks on a first-time inmate in solitary had been carried out, if they had then she would still be alive now.

The jangling of the keys roused me from my dozing, my repaired copy of The Republic resting on my chest, and I quickly got off my bunk and stood hands behind my back, flat against the rear wall as a solitary guard entered my cell.

'Taylor. Dress. Now. Then come with me' growled the guard

'Where are we going, Miss?' I enquired

I was told to get dressed and given an ill-fitting two-piece suit and forced my feet into a pair of shoes that had perhaps once been worn by a large child. They were so tight I could only manage to sort of shuffle and walk behind the guard but eventually found myself at the guard room.

'Miss. Can you please tell me where I am going?'

'You can ask Taylor, or you can shut the fuck up and sign this' they said as the guard shoved a form in front of me.

I had no time to read it and so just signed it and was then handcuffed and placed in a waiting van. The van sped out of the centre's gates whilst the driver repeatedly reminded me

'If I'm fucking late off because of you Taylor, there will be fucking trouble, you hear?'

I kept apologising but he wouldn't tell me where I was going and as the van raced along the winding streets I tried to make out where we were and what my final destination would be. It couldn't be a prison transfer; I would have been allowed to bring all my belongings with me. It couldn't be my trial, that was months away and my solicitor had only seen me yesterday. No, this was something out of the ordinary, something brought before the courts at the last minute perhaps. Were there extra charges to be brought against me? Had my other crimes been added to the current ones? Oh, this was not good, not good at all.

After twenty minutes of being flung about in the rear of the van and twenty minutes of trying to keep down today's culinary delight of shepherd's pie, vegetables, and semolina (not all together you understand) the van jerked to a halt and the doors were flung open

'Out !' though my chauffeur offered me no hand to assist me down from my carriage

I came out into the light and blinked at the brightness. Something kept flashing in front of me and it took me a little while to realise it was a flashbulb going off.

Someone was taking my picture, oh what must I have looked like. Ill-fitting suit, even worse shoes and my hair was just a mess. Still, Vogue, here I am if you want me.

I was grabbed forcibly by the elbow and ushered through the crowd. I hadn't seen so many people all in one place for some time, perhaps ever, and it was frightening I can tell you. People were shouting questions at me, but I couldn't hear what they were asking, and I said nothing except, 'sorry, sorry, excuse me' as I was forced through the hoard of assembled people.

I was taken down to the cell area and told to wait until someone came for me.
About an hour later the door opened and my solicitor entered. He sat next to me on the cell bench and smiling, spoke to me. My 'solicitor', a man known to me as Malcolm Bastwick, but known to the legal profession as Martin
Bentham said

MB   Cath. We have some very good news for you today. You are to be released
CT   What? How? Why? What's happened? Released, when?

MB   Well, that's quite a lot of questions so let me answer them in turn. You are to be released. How? All charges have been put before the court and due to time served you are to be released. The when, well that will be later on, today. After the hearing you will be taken back to the remand centre for a bit of paperwork, but I will follow you there. Then I will take you anywhere you want to go….as a free woman. Is that about everything?

CT   Martin …I mean Malcolm, I don't understand. You're not even a solicitor? How has this happened

MB   Ah. Malcolm Bastwick may not be a solicitor, but Martin Bentham is, or rather he used to be, but I am no longer Martin Bentham, I am now Malcolm Bastwick, or is it the other way around, I can't remember. Anyway, I may have been in correspondence with the court, or perhaps Martin Bentham's headed paperwork has been received by the court. Either way they have accepted that due to all the corruption at the police station and your invaluable help in taking down some very sought-after scalps, they are prepared

to say the time you have spent on remand
is equal to the sentence you would
have received.

CT   But how can that be? I stole five hundred
thousand pounds worth of cash

MB   Ah. No. Actually you didn't. You stole
counterfeit notes the face value of which
was five hundred thousand pounds. None
of it was real.

CT   What? Yes, it was, I looked, I saw, I
swapped every note over in the bags

MB   You needn't have bothered. None of it
was real. What you took out of the police
station   was   worthless   paper.   What
happened to that worthless paper after that
is none of your concern.

CT   But,   and   purely   hypothetically   you
understand

MB   Of course - you can trust me I am, well I
was a solicitor

CT   What if all those notes were paid into
bank accounts?

MB   Well, hypothetically they would all be
absorbed   into   the   wonderful   banking
system and be of value…hypothetically

CT   Of value?

MB   Indeed. Now, there are some people waiting to see you when you are freed. They gave character references for you. I think they'll be pleased to see you, Cath.

CT   Thank you Malcolm. But you've changed, you used to be…well, odd. I haven't been away that long, how have you changed so much

MB   It's because of you Dorcas. Do you remember when we sat in that interview room, all three of us?

CT   Two, Malcolm, there were only two of us

MB   I know, I'm just pulling your leg, Dorcas. I knew I had to change, most of what I was like was an act anyway, but you were kind to me. You didn't ridicule me like most other people did

CT   No. Of course not, why would I?

MB   You wouldn't, but others did, and that just made me more cross, more confused in my thinking. So, I changed. I do actually know quite a lot about the law, you know from reading and so on, oh, and when I used to be Martin Bentham. And I do intend to go legit again one day…just not yet.

CT   Well that's wonderful . And I have to change as well. Dorcas has gone Malcolm. I can't be Dorcas anymore. I liked her, of all my names, I really liked her, but she has gone. For me to continue I need to move on. I will think of something, someone else. I will come back again. In a while though, I need a break.

MB   Oh, that reminds me. I have something for you - here

Malcolm then gave me an envelope inside which was a key and a postcard of a place I knew very well, Alopece, just outside Athens - it was the birthplace of my favourite man in the whole world - Socrates.

The postcard read:-

Dorcas,

Go back to where your hero began his life, where you can begin yours again.

Take the enclosed key to the post office and use what you find wisely.

It was signed

Pete

Travels

I returned to the remand centre and collected all my belongings - my clothes, my books and especially all the pictures from my wall.

I said goodbye to the place that I had called home for a while and had briefly shared with Carole and as I turned my back on prison life for good, I wondered what she would have been like if she had survived. Carole had intrigued me from the start. I hadn't liked her for much of the time I had known her, but she was complicated and, as it turned out, she was a lot deeper than she let on. I wondered if we would have eventually become friends, had things been different. I would never know.

Malcolm was true to his word and took me to the airport. I boarded a plane, as Cath Taylor, bound for Athens and contemplated my next move.
I was, in my mind anyway, going back home, to my hero's birthplace as Pete had said. How had she known that Athens was everything to me, my sanctuary, my religion almost.

As we flew over warm seas and the coastline approached, I took out the postcard and compared it in my mind with the picture Carole had kept on her wall. Was it the same place? Could Carole and Frank have been in Athens when that loving picture was taken, again, it was something I would never know.

But for now, I thought, I must rest. I had had a few years of running, and I now desperately wanted to rest, to put my feet up and enjoy a little 'me time' as they say, and where better than Greece?

I was in Athens for two weeks; Malcolm having arranged for my ticket and my stay at a little hotel just out of the town. I was biding my time before going to the Post Office. I didn't know if it was a trick or why all the subterfuge, but I couldn't afford to get caught in something criminal here.

The day before I was due to come home, I plucked up the courage and walked into the 'Post Office'. It was a small airless place with a shop at the front that sold all the usual tourist bits and pieces, whilst at the back there was….nothing.
I asked the man behind the counter if there was an actual Post Office here to which he nodded

and smiled, but then again, I think I could have asked him anything and he would have nodded and smiled. He did not speak English very well and my Greek was , well, non-existent.

I had no other choice and so I pulled the key from the pocket of my shorts and waved it in the air like it should open something. At this the man nodded and smiled, what else would he do, but then he beckoned me towards the rear of the shop.

Out of immediate sight was a group of lockers - the sort of things you'd have at a swimming pool or at a bus station. Each locker was numbered and holding my breath I matched my key with a locker - could it be really that simple?
I thanked the shopkeeper in my best non-Greek and waited until he had gone back behind his counter.

I tried the key in the lock, fearing it would not turn, but it did. I opened the locker door and found another envelope. What was it with all the envelopes?
Inside the envelope was a birth certificate and a piece of paper with numbers on it. 40 23 45 00167668 - a bank account surely?

I looked at the birth certificate but did not recognise the name, but a smaller piece of paper attached to it explained everything, and I couldn't believe what it said.

The following day I waited at the airport, mystified as to what the bank account was, who it belonged to and what it was to do with me. The name of the birth certificate had stumped me, and I didn't know if that was who I really was, or whether it belonged to someone else. Certainly, the surname was unfamiliar to me but for some reason not the first name.

Coming home at last

Having returned from Greece I went to the only person I knew that worked in a bank, my friend Trevor. I needed his help to work out what was going on. I queued with all the other bank customers and eventually found myself at the till. Trevor was walking past on his way to his office and stopped, open mouthed

T   Cath? Is that you? What are you doing here, is everything OK? Please tell me that everything is, OK?

CT   Oh yes Trevor, never better, though I could do with your help. If you have a minute?

T   Yes. Yes, come through to my office. Cup of tea?

CT   Lovely, thank you

And so, we sat and reminisced about old times. He delicately avoided the subject of me going to prison, and I delicately avoided reminding him that he owed me a favour.

I showed Trevor the piece of paper and he entered the numbers into his computer.

T   Fuck me , Cath. Is this yours? I mean, sorry. Is this your account?
CT   I don't know, I'm not sure. I think so, but I don't know who's name it's in
T   Cath. I can't just tell you that, I mean, do you have anything with a name on it at all, anything to link this account to you?

I showed him the birth certificate and as it matched the name on the account, he span the computer round and showed me what had stunned him into an expletive he didn't normally use in front of me.

The name of the account was Ophelia Albright and the account held just over five hundred thousand pounds in it. Sister Ophelia had been one of the original Sisters at the children's home I had lived in - was this a sign?

Peace

You will be pleased to know that I am coming to the end of my story. There's only a little bit left, so please bear with me.

Having been given access to five hundred thousand pounds I did the only thing I could think of doing with that sum of money. I opened a children's home - oh not a council run, underfunded, dilapidated place - although that's what it had been when I lived there. No, my new venture was a place for people, including me, to call a proper home. I purchased the old shut down children's home and made it into something wonderful, something I could be proud of.

I managed to find two excellent teachers to educate the waifs and strays who came here - their names were Kerry and Emma and they each had their own room at my home, rent free and unencumbered by landlords overstaying their welcome.

For security, especially at night, I had a former would-be Drugs Squad detective and dog handler called Larry. He hadn't liked being in the police after all and even with a change of role he couldn't settle and so he jumped at the chance of helping me out. We often have a toasted cheese sandwich and a cup of tea late into the night and talk about old times.

I had Pete come and set up the grounds and erect a greenhouse at the back of the property - there's something comforting about having plants around you that makes things just seem so much more homely. He is also my business advisor, and I have Trevor to help and guide me with all things to do with banking and investments.

Apparently between the two of them, whilst I was otherwise engaged you understand, they managed to launder the counterfeit notes, all five hundred thousand pounds worth of them through all the accounts Pete had set up and then on to Ophelia Albright's account at Trevor's bank. It sort of has a completeness to it, don't you think?

I now sit in my office, and survey all around me and I think I am truly happy, maybe for the first time in my life, certainly for the longest time in my life. I have come back to where it all started for me, I have come home. To a place I will call home until I am no more.

I have been many people throughout my life.
I was born an unknown, deposited by people
I never met and named following a nun's hat lottery. I became Catherine Taylor, gained a Philosophy degree, and later was imprisoned for fraud, though they never found where that money went either.

Then I became Dorcas, an invisible cleaner, ignored by people who thought they were important, while she went about her work, perhaps God's work (there Sister Bernadette, I've said it) and hopefully someone who will be remembered not for the bad that they did, but for the good. I liked Dorcas and I wish her well, wherever she is. And remember there are many such as her all over the place and goodness knows what they are really doing as they mop and sweep, dust, and polish.

And now I am Sister Ophelia, a Catholic nun returned from overseas. Don't worry, there is a back story, every fraudster needs a back story that will hold up under scrutiny, but my days of being a fraudster, being someone I am not, are over, apart from the nun bit.

Oh? The name Albright. Yes. I nearly forgot......Pete made it up - it was the name of one of the cleaners who didn't exist but worked so hard and did all that overtime, and I sort of liked it. I felt comfortable using it as my own. It wasn't as nice as Dorcas Goode, but I was happy with it.

As I look out of the window, I see our gardener and handyman. He looks different now, happier. I tap on the glass

'Vita est bonum' I ask - is life good?

'Vita valde bona gratias ago tibi, Sister Ophelia' he replies. Life is very good, thank you

Smart arse, Latin degree holding, former Custody Sergeant that he is.

Printed in Great Britain
by Amazon

19473000R00173